All You Get Is Me

Also by Yvonne Prinz

All You Get Is Me

Yvonne Prinz

HARPER TEEN
An Imprint of HarperCollinsPublishers

HarperTeen is an imprint of HarperCollins Publishers.

All You Get Is Me
Copyright © 2011 by Yvonne Prinz
All rights reserved. Printed in the United States of America.
No part of this book may be used or reproduced in any manner
whatsoever without written permission except in the case of brief
quotations embodied in critical articles and reviews.
For information address HarperCollins Children's Books,
a division of HarperCollins Publishers, 10 East 53rd Street,
New York, NY 10022.
www.harperteen.com

Library of Congress Cataloging-in-Publication Data
Prinz, Yvonne.
All you get is me / Yvonne Prinz. — 1st ed.
   p. cm.
Summary: Almost sixteen-year-old city-transplant Aurora must
adapt to life on an organic farm as she navigates an eventful summer
when she falls in love, discovers that her mother has left for good,
and watches her father take a bold stand in defense of the rights of
undocumented Mexican farmworkers.
   ISBN 978-0-06-171580-8
   [1. Farm life—California—Fiction. 2. Mexicans—United States—
Fiction. 3. Migrant labor—Fiction. 4. Illegal aliens—Fiction.
5. Dating (Social customs)—Fiction. 6. Grief—Fiction. 7. California—
Fiction.] I. Title.
PZ7.P93678Al 2011   2010007822
[Fic]—dc22   CIP
                                                               AC

Typography by Alison Klapthor
11 12 13 14 15 LP/RRDB 10 9 8 7 6 5 4 3 2 1
❖
First Edition

For Rick and Kristie Knoll of Knoll Farms in Brentwood, California, who inspired this story

Just before the crash, I was watching you
Thinking how time hasn't changed
Even half of what it promised to

—Joe Henry

1

*M*y mom always promised me she would keep me safe, and then she disappeared.

My dad made no such promise.

Five a.m. on a Tuesday morning, mere days after school has let out for summer vacation and I'm already getting into a delicious groove of sleeping late. I'm cruelly torn from a deep, luxurious sleep by my dad, pounding on my bedroom door.

"C'mon, honey, up and at 'em."

No. NO! Go away. My cheek is resting comfortably on my pillow in a warm puddle of drool and I've completely forgotten that I'm working the market today. Why did I say I would do that?

"Roar?" He says my name now, knocking lightly.

"Okay, okay, I'm up," I mumble.

I hear his leather boots on the old wooden stairs leading down to the kitchen. I slide out of bed, one limb at a time. One foot hits the cool plank floor, then the other. The farmhouse is chilly right now, but as the day wears on, the early summer warmth will creep slowly into all the corners of this house. It never gets really hot in here, though; we're protected by an ancient, enormous oak tree that leans over the old roof with its muscular arms providing much-needed shade in the long, hot afternoons to come. The same tree also diabolically twists its gnarled roots into our plumbing so that every couple of months muddy brown water bubbles up through the drains and into all of the sinks and the claw-foot bathtub upstairs. It's beyond gross. We have Jesus, our Roto-Rooter man, on speed dial.

Rufus butts the bedroom door open with his snout and clicks across the wood planks to say good morning. He's an early riser and a fantastic afternoon napper. Bits of dog food cling to his mongrel beard. He nuzzles my face with his nose and I ruffle the fur on his soft head, which smells slightly of skunk. Rufus is a country dog. I am a city girl. Rufus has lived here on the farm all of his life and I have lived in the city all of mine until two years ago last spring when my dad up and bought a farm like he was running out for a quart of milk. I'm pretty sure I'll never forgive him for that.

I stand up, yawning and stretching, and peer out my bedroom window into the darkness. It looks like midnight except for a ribbon of pale blue marking the horizon. A light shines over the gravel driveway next to the house. The old brown pickup (like Rufus, it came with the place) is parked there, weighed down with our early summer vegetables and fruit: fava beans, dandelion greens, fennel, green garlic, arugula, baby potatoes, and the first of the apricots. Steve and Miguel and my dad loaded it after it cooled off last night. Steve, a UC Berkeley grad student, fast-talked his way out of doing his regular farmers' market shift because he and his girlfriend, Jane, are going rafting on the American River. This is Steve's second summer working with us, and lucky for him, I'm completely in love with him so I said I'd cover for him today. He promised me a mix CD featuring some indie bands he's been listening to.

Out beyond the apricot orchard, which is thickly planted between the knobby trees with garlic, runner beans, and horseradish, a light burns in the window of the bunkhouse that Miguel and Steve share. My dad fashioned it out of one of the several outbuildings on the property. It gets pretty hot in there by August but Steve's from the desert and Miguel's from Oaxaca, Mexico, so they're both pretty okay with the heat. Steve is here from late May till late August, and Miguel is here until he saves enough money to buy a little piece of land back in Mexico to build a home on. Miguel sends almost every penny he makes home to his wife, Magdelena, and his two boys, Carlos and Marco. Their photos are Scotch-taped next to the pillow in his bunk. Carlos and Marco have bright dark eyes and matching wide grins with big teeth and ears that they haven't grown into yet and Magdelena smiles shyly and wears a delicate gold crucifix on a chain around her neck.

My dad is crashing around the small kitchen, preparing his standard breakfast: a giant latte (featuring organic local milk and fair trade coffee that he buys from an Italian guy in North Beach who roasts his beans to perfection) and a big bowl of granola from Sally and Jim, our half-crazy neighbors up the road who make it from scratch and sell it to health food stores. My dad trades them for apricots, which they dry for the cereal. As I brush my teeth and pull my hair into a ponytail, I can hear Dad foaming the milk on the espresso machine, a monster of a thing, left over from our life in the city. It takes up most of the counter space in our kitchen and cost us about as much as our secondhand tractor. Of course, I never even used to think about the cost of things till we became farmers. Now everything comes down to that.

"Hey, sport," my dad says way too cheerfully when I

appear in the doorway of the kitchen. "Can I fry you an egg or two?"

I shake my head. "I'll just have toast. I don't want to wake up too much."

I slice a big chunk off a loaf of bread and wedge it into the toaster. My dad hands me a jar of homemade strawberry jam from the fridge, the kind where you can still see the whole strawberries. When the toast pops up, the edges are burnt. I slather it with butter and jam and sit down at the old table. My dad pours me a glass of orange juice and sits down across from me. National Public Radio drifts in from the stereo in the living room. Rufus curls up under the table and we both use him as a footstool. I bury my bare feet in his soft fur and he groans. I crunch my toast and my dad slurps his latte and spoons granola into his mouth while he reads yesterday's *New York Times*. He won't get today's until this afternoon. Country life.

I glance at a brochure from a solar panel company sitting on the table next to a jar of honey. My dad has ordered solar panels for the roof of the barn but we probably won't get them up until after the summer growing season because the roof needs repairs. Once they're up we'll have enough free power to run the tristate area but we'll probably be paying off the panels forever.

At six o'clock we finally get ourselves out to the truck,

which doubles as my dad's office. Papers and receipts are stacked under both visors, and the dusty seat is littered with clipboards, pens, CDs, a carrot, a screwdriver, and a baseball cap. I put my camera down on the seat between us. It's a Nikon FM with a Nikkor thirty-five-millimeter lens. I don't go anywhere without it. My dad slips his insulated coffee cup into a carrier he installed in the dash, above the stereo that he also installed. He pulled it out of the old black Mercedes sedan that he drove in his pre-farm days, which is now gathering dust and pigeon poop in the barn. He says I can have it when I learn to drive. What he doesn't know is that I already know how. Steve taught me in his Jeep. I just need a license, which I'll get the minute I'm sixteen, two months from now.

My dad starts the truck and it groans to life. He grinds the gearshift into reverse and we back out and roll past the farmhouse on the gravel driveway. Even though the pretty flowered kitchen curtains ruffle in the breeze, the house still always looks to me like the house in a southern Gothic thriller. The kind where the farmer goes insane and everybody ends up dead with a pitchfork through the brain.

The sun is all the way up now and Miguel already has the tractor out.

He's hooked up a flatbed trailer to the back of it and he's heading out to the vegetable patch. Steve's Jeep is already gone. My dad pulls up next to Miguel and asks him in Spanish if he can collect the eggs from the chicken coop and let the chickens out. They roam free during the day, eating bugs and pooping everywhere. Every organic farmer knows that chicken poop is the best fertilizer on earth. The chickens are my chore but I've been spared today. The coop is off behind the barn and it smells like sweet rotting grain, and even though I feed them every day, the chickens seem to resent me. I've given them beautiful names like Gretta and Frieda and Mona and Astrid. I praise their work, the simple perfection of the eggs they lay, but I get nothing from them. It's like they know I'm a fake. I don't belong here and they're onto me. Luckily Rufus doesn't share their dim view of me and he trots along beside the truck like a Secret Service guy running next to the president's motorcade, ready to take a bullet for me.

Miguel calls out "Adios" to me and waves. He calls me by my full name, Aurora. Everyone else calls me Roar. I wave back. We stop at the entrance to the farm and pull out onto the road that will eventually take us to the freeway. Rufus stops there and watches us disappear before he turns around and heads inside for a nap. I'm pretty sure that my dad and Steve have a lot to talk about on these long drives. They have tons in common, even though Steve's a lot younger than my dad. They're both very political and love to talk about how this country's going to hell in a hand-basket, but they can go from that directly to which Jimi Hendrix album rocks the hardest.

No such luck with me. I start to doze almost immediately. Tom Waits is playing on the stereo. He's singing "Hold On." It's beautiful and sad. My head bobs along with the rocking of the old truck as my dad navigates his way along the winding road. He and Steve do the Ferry Plaza Farmers Market in San Francisco twice a week, so my dad knows every bump and curve in the road.

I jerk awake to the sound of my dad cursing. "Goddamn development people!" he says, watching his side mirror nervously.

I look in the mirror on my side of the truck. An SUV is behind us, inches from our rear bumper. A blond woman is at the wheel and she's honking her horn. There's no shoulder on this road and it's full of sharp turns and blind corners. Since they started building housing developments on some of the land north of us there've been a lot more people using this road. My dad, a man with a big opinion about everything, considers the development people to be sort of an alien invasion, a blight on the land in the form of Costco-shopping, SUV-driving breeders, people who have to commute hours to the surrounding cities just to go to work. He believes that humans have lost their way in the world, that they're so far removed from the land that they don't even recognize it when they see it anymore. Pretty big talk for a guy who became a farmer about twenty minutes ago. The small farmers around here have started organizing themselves against the developers, with my dad at the helm. He knows that zoning laws are quietly being manipulated to accommodate the builders and he's not about to sit still for it. When we lived in the city, my dad was a human rights lawyer, so trust me, no one's better at getting up in your face than he is. Still, even though they enjoy the occasional victory, it's mostly a losing battle here and all over the country as farmland is being sold off to developers because farmers are giving up the struggle to survive.

The woman behind us is getting more and more agitated by the second. In my mirror I can see her lips forming curse words and her manicured fingernails death-gripping the steering wheel.

We approach a short straightaway, which is followed by a curve that dips down into a valley of dense forest for about half a mile. The SUV pulls out from behind us to pass, crossing a double solid yellow line. As it approaches the driver's side of the pickup my dad touches his brakes to let her pass but she slows down as their windows line up and gives my dad the finger. I watch her hateful sneering face and I think, *Lady, you may live to regret that.* As she turns her attention back to the road I see her face change to horror as an oncoming pickup truck appears on the road directly in front of her. My dad swerves off the road and slams on his brakes but there's nowhere for him to go. We watch, frozen, as the woman yanks her steering wheel hard to the right, narrowly missing the front of my dad's truck, and slams almost head-on into the oncoming pickup. The noise is unbearable. The pickup whips around, changing directions, and its back end flips over the embankment into a small ravine. The truck comes to rest upside down with all four wheels still spinning. Tom Waits is singing about getting behind the mule. The SUV has rolled over too and skids to a stop in the middle of the road. Suddenly it's dead quiet.

My dad throws the truck into park and digs his cell phone out of his shirt pocket. He thrusts it at me.

"Roar, call 9-1-1. Tell them where we are. Tell them it's bad, okay?"

My dad runs across the road to the edge of the ravine and surveys the wreck.

My hands shake uncontrollably as I press the numbers into his phone. I give the annoyingly calm emergency operator our information in a trembling voice and I beg her to tell them to hurry. She tells me that help is on the way and I should stay on the line till it arrives. It's all I can do not to scream, "HURRY UP!"

My dad has lowered himself down the edge of the ravine and he's making his way to the passenger side of the truck. A baby is hanging upside down in a car seat. My dad jimmies the door open and the baby starts to cry. He undoes the buckles and grabs her to keep her from falling. I take the phone and sit on the edge of the ravine. I won't let myself look at the driver's side.

"Is she okay?" I ask.

"I think so." He takes her into his arms. She's plump and dark skinned, wearing a pretty little sundress with a few drops of blood down the front. My dad scrambles up the bank with her. She's calm now and she seems to be okay. He hands her to me. I put her in my lap and rock her a bit, telling her everything will be all right even though I'm pretty sure it won't. I wipe the tears off her cheeks with the sleeve of my sweatshirt. She searches my face with her big dark eyes, trying to figure out if she knows me. I check her for injuries but all I can find is a greenish blue goose egg on her forehead. I glance over at the SUV. The driver isn't moving and there's a trickle of blood on her forehead.

After what seems like a lifetime but is actually a couple of minutes, I hear the wail of sirens. I tell the operator they've arrived and hang up the phone. By that time my dad has worked his way over to the driver's side of the overturned truck and he's talking to the driver, a woman, in Spanish and holding her hand. The paramedics leap into action. One of them gently takes the baby away from me. She starts to cry again. A policeman pulls up behind the ambulance and a fire truck follows him. The cop deals with the cars that are starting to back up behind the accident and the firemen assess the scene and pull out a stretcher to lower into the ravine. The paramedics work on the SUV driver. They pull a gurney over to her and attach a cervical collar around her neck before they ease her onto it.

My dad scrambles back down the ravine, next to the stretcher, and speaks quietly to the woman as they maneuver her out of the ravine. He tells her that her baby is fine and that she'll be fine too. Her eyes are closed and I can't tell if she's breathing. Her left arm is crushed and she looks like she's lost a lot of blood. We stand there helpless and watch them load her into the ambulance. My dad turns to me, wiping tears from his eyes. There's a smear of blood on his cheek.

"Roar. Go get your camera."

"Is she going to be okay?"

"I don't think so. Go get your camera and take some pictures of the truck and the SUV, okay?"

"Okay." I run to the truck and grab my camera. It's loaded with black-and-white film and I've got about half a roll of film left. My dad distracts the cop, explaining what

12

happened, and I shoot off the rest of the roll. I get the mangled truck, the SUV, long shots and close-ups. I don't photograph the victims, though. I won't do that.

The police want my dad to come down to the station and file a full report but he says he wants to go to the hospital first to see how the woman is doing. They seem okay with that and one of them takes down his information on a little notepad. We climb into the truck and drive slowly to the hospital, arriving long after the ambulance. The scene where the doctors yell and the nurses grab at things that can jolt a person back to life is all over by the time we get there. The police from the scene are wrapping things up in that overly officious way they have of making you feel guilty even if you haven't done anything. On their way out they remind my dad about coming to the station and I can see his back go up. He's never been great with cops.

The waiting room is calm again, perched for its next disaster. My dad talks his way into where the woman and her baby are. I sit down in a turquoise vinyl chair and try to watch late-breaking CNN news on the TV mounted above me because it's a whole lot better than the image of the accident that keeps creeping back into my head. My hands are still shaking, my throat is tight, and tears keep rolling down my cheeks. Every few minutes I look anxiously at the double doors that my dad disappeared behind. The receptionist looks up at me sympathetically. I wipe my face on my sleeve. She decides not to say anything. This isn't the first time I've been to this emergency room. You wouldn't even believe the things that can go wrong when you live on a farm. I have a scar on my knuckle from accidentally putting my hand through a glass window in the barn. I had to get seven stitches. That was a mess. Another time I was here with my dad and Steve when Steve fell out of the hayloft on his ankle. He had to get it X-rayed. He says he slipped. I think he was stoned. I read a story once about a farmer who severed both arms in a piece of farm machinery and he actually had the presence of mind to dial 9-1-1 with a pencil in his mouth. You've really got to hand it to that guy. I think they even put his arms back on.

The glass doors hiss open and a man in an expensive suit and important-looking shoes strides into the waiting room and makes a beeline for the receptionist. She looks up again with a face that says "Don't mess with me." She has a name tag that says "Candy" pinned to her enormous bosom. A kid who looks about a year older than me trails behind Mr. Slick. He's wearing the opposite outfit: a torn Misfits T-shirt, baggy jeans, and worn-out Converse sneakers. His thick black hair hangs in his eyes and I suspect he may hate everyone, especially Mr. Slick, who is now speaking to Candy in a very loud voice as though she might be hearing-impaired.

"My wife was brought in here, Connie Gilwood. She was in a car accident. I need to see her immediately. Where is she?"

Candy seems not to appreciate his tone. "Let me just locate her, sir," she says tersely. She types efficiently on a keyboard and clicks a mouse.

"Just tell me where she is, damn it!" He clutches a cell phone in his hand and he seems to be thinking about hurling it at her.

The kid, who I now know is the son of the woman who was driving the SUV, shuffles his feet and looks at the floor.

"Sir," says Candy, "I'm here to help but that kind of talk generally doesn't inspire me to move any faster."

"Well, there must be someone else I can talk to—a doctor, a manager?"

Candy points to her name tag. Underneath her name it says "Emergency Room Supervisor."

"I'm it, darling," she says, smirking at him.

The kid's eyes meet mine and he looks away, embarrassed.

"Okay, here she is, Connie Gilwood." She reads from a computer monitor. "She's doing just fine. I'm assuming you're Mr. Gilwood?" She looks over her reading glasses at him.

Just as she says the name, the double doors that separate the waiting room from the drama swing wide and my dad appears.

"You're Mr. Gilwood?" he asks Mr. Slick.

"Yeah. You know about my wife?"

"I sure do." My dad's voice is shaking a bit. "Your wife is fine. The woman she hit was just pronounced dead. There's a baby back there without a mother." He points behind him with his thumb.

"Who the hell are you?" Mr. Slick takes in my dad's ponytail and his dirty jeans and his flannel shirt.

"You'll know soon enough." He heads for the exit. "C'mon, Roar," he says, but I'm already there. I look back over my shoulder at the son. He's watching my dad with something in his eyes that I can't quite read. It definitely isn't shock, though.

The sliding glass doors hiss open again and we walk out into the midmorning sunlight.

2

My mother started to slip away from us when I was ten. We lived in a tall, narrow Victorian house on Church Street in Noe Valley, a quiet neighborhood in San Francisco. If you go to the corner of Church and Twenty-fourth streets and turn right, you can walk down a long, steep hill that leads to the Mission District. I wasn't allowed to go there on my own but my dad and I would walk down the hill together. We wandered through the fragrant produce stalls and bought weird stuff like plantains and jicama and sweet mangoes. Sometimes we'd walk all the way down Twenty-fourth to the Roosevelt Tamale Parlor for the best tamales in town. I would drink lemonade and my dad would drink dark Mexican beer. If it was summer, we'd walk up San Jose Avenue to Mitchell's Ice Cream and try to outweird each other with our flavor choices. Mitchell's is about a thousand years old and features exotic flavors like avocado and purple yam.

Our house was a lively place back then. My mom was a painter and she hosted dinners for all her artist friends and they brought their friends and then my dad would show up with all his left-wing activist friends. The parties went late into the night and no one ever thought to send me to bed. I usually fell asleep on the sofa with music and dancing and strange accents swirling around me. Eventually my dad would throw me over his shoulder and carry me off to my bedroom, where I would sleep through the noise. My mom would come in later and kiss me, smelling of wine and her spicy perfume.

My mom painted most days in a light-filled room at the front of the house, overlooking our street. She could look out the bay window and watch the Church Street trolley roll by. For a while she was happy all the time. There was lots of laughter in our house back then as she told stories about her day and then eagerly wanted to hear about ours as she moved about the kitchen, making dinner. Eventually it became clear that her art was never going to sell. The people she went to art school with were getting their own gallery shows and selling their work but no one seemed too keen on my mom's paintings of flying pigs and Dalmatians and cows. Eventually, even my mom seemed to lose interest in her own work and most afternoons I would come home from school at three to find her passed out on the big burgundy velvet sofa in her studio with an empty wine bottle on the table next to her.

My dad had his hands full defending people who couldn't defend themselves. Most of those people couldn't afford to pay much either, but he never put pressure on my mom to get a real job. He was crazy about her and he would come home dead tired at night and sit next to her on the sofa, rubbing her arm and kissing her, trying to breathe some life into her, but she would just lie there like a rag doll or tell him to go away. My dad, who was never much of a cook, learned to make simple dishes like lentil soup and stew. Usually it was just the two of us at the table.

The parties at our house stopped and invitations to parties at other artists' houses stopped too. My mother, once the life of the party, had become an embarrassment. She drank too much and spewed bitterness about the politics of the art world. She often ended up in tears and my dad would have to apologize to everyone and then help her out to the car. I could hear him on the phone, late at night, talking to Jacob, his best friend from college, trying to figure out how to help her, how to get her back. Jacob is a psychiatrist and he prescribed antidepressants, but my mom wasn't supposed to take them if she was drinking so she didn't take them at all.

My mom started to lose weight. Bit by bit, her curvy figure and her Black Irish features disappeared. Her shiny black hair grew dull and thin and her bright blue eyes turned gray and empty. My dad and I started treating her like a piece of furniture, passing her on our way out somewhere with barely a glance in her direction. I raided her closet and started wearing her clothes to school. I safety-pinned the waistbands of her colorful gypsy skirts to fit me and I wore a bunch of beaded necklaces at once around my neck and wrapped her silk shawls around me. At school, no one seemed to notice. I went to the kind of school that encourages free expression. There was no such thing as a red flag when it came to a kid's wardrobe choices.

Some mornings, my mom would stagger out of bed and make pancakes for us. She seemed almost like her old self again, chattering away or humming happily to gypsy guitar music on the stereo. My dad and I played along, complimenting her cooking even though the pancakes were either burnt or gooey and raw in the middle. On those days, I would come home to find my mom back in her spot, the sink full of the breakfast dishes and the milk going sour on the counter next to an open box of eggs and a bag of pancake mix.

Even in this condition, my mom tried really hard to be

the kind of mom she thought I needed. She would show up for parent-teacher meetings with smeared makeup and rumpled clothes and alcohol on her breath until I started hiding the letters from school.

One afternoon I came home from school to find her gone. The sofa was empty except for the indentation of my now-petite mother's body on the burgundy velvet. I called around to all her old friends but no one had seen her in months. When my dad got home, we drove around the neighborhood, checking in bars and coffeehouses and bookstores, but we came home hours later, exhausted, without her.

At three a.m. the police called. They'd found her slumped over on a bus bench on Castro Street and taken her to the hospital. We went to pick her up. She was drunk and dehydrated and she had a few bruises on her but otherwise she was okay. My dad signed the release form and helped her into the car. No one said anything on the ride home. My mom looked out the window.

The next morning my mom was up and dressed in jeans, which now hung on her. She had blue-green bags under her eyes, and a bruise on her cheek had swelled into a bump. She buzzed around the kitchen like she'd been slapped awake and told she had to play the part of the mother in a production of *We're a Normal Family*. When I emerged from my bedroom in my pajamas she kissed me like she hadn't seen me in months.

"Roar, honey," she said, placing her hands on my shoulders and looking me in the eyes, "things are going to be different from now on. I promise. I'm better now. I really am."

Mom never told us what happened out there that night but it must have given her a jolt because she kept up the perfect mom/loving wife act for a couple of weeks. She even agreed to enter a rehab program. My dad and I held our breath. A week later she was back on the sofa and a week after that she started disappearing again. At first it was overnight, then it was a few days at a time. Sometimes she would show up on her own and sometimes the police would bring her home or the hospital would call. One day she disappeared for good. My dad filed a missing-persons report and he drove all over the city every night, looking for her in neighborhoods and places he'd never even been before. He hired a private investigator who came up empty. He told us that some people just don't want to be found. My dad wouldn't give up. He searched on the internet for my mom's mother and finally found her in Vermont. Shortly after they met, my mom had told my dad that she'd had a falling-out with her mother and hadn't spoken to her in years, and that her dad was dead. Her mom, my grandmother, told us that no such falling-out had happened and that my mom's dad was very much alive. She said that my mom had just up and disappeared one day, never contacting them to tell them where she'd gone. My dad put me on the phone. They didn't even know they had a grandchild. Her voice reminded me a bit of my mom's. We had an awkward conversation and then I put my dad back on. He cried when he said good-bye to them and promised to keep them posted.

Through all of this I never hated my mom. I couldn't very well hate someone who'd taught me how to polka, someone who'd taught me how to read tea leaves, give butterfly kisses, and make butterscotch brownies. When I was six, she gave me a Pentax point-and-shoot camera and taught me how to take a picture. I took photos of everything. Those photos are in a box in my bedroom closet now except for the best ones of my mom. Those I framed. They sit on my desk, pictures of her laughing at the beach, in the kitchen, walking up the street, painting. I got a better camera for my tenth birthday, with a zoom lens. I became a more accomplished photographer but I never got a great photo of my mom. She'd started slipping away by then. Now I never go anywhere without my camera.

After my mom disappeared for the last time, we left everything just the way it was for a whole year, even the paints, brushes, and canvases. We didn't touch anything.

We couldn't. During that year I saw my mom everywhere: in bookstores, coffee shop windows, standing in line for movie tickets. But it was my old mom, back when she was happy and beautiful. I would even walk toward her, ready for her to smile at me and take me into her arms, but it was never her. Every afternoon when I came home from school, I half expected to find her there in the studio, painting or watching the world go by on Church Street. But eventually we realized we were waiting for something that was never going to happen. My dad packed up all her art supplies and her paintings into boxes and put them in our storage closet downstairs. One afternoon, not long after that, he picked me up at school and told me that we were moving on with our lives.

"What does that mean?" I asked.

"It means we're moving."

"Moving? Where to?"

"A farm. We're moving to a farm."

"We're going to live with farmers?"

"No. We *are* the farmers."

3

*T*hirteen black-and-white photos of the accident hang across the clothesline in my darkroom like crime-scene laundry. The last one is still in the developing solution. I push it around with rubber-tipped bamboo tongs as the image comes into focus. It's the overturned SUV resting in the middle of the asphalt road. In the upper right-hand corner is an unintentional piece of the ambulance with its back doors open. I must have taken it right after the paramedics loaded the stretchers. Sylvia Hernandez's bare foot is clearly visible. You can also see part of her other foot, which somehow still has a pristine white sneaker on it. I remove the print from the developer and drop it in the stop bath. I can't take my eyes off Sylvia's foot. Next to the accident photos are the rest of the photos from the roll: a Buddhist monk with a shaved head eating a wedge of melon, a young, smiling monk holding a puppy, Steve trying to hypnotize a chicken, a three-legged dog. I took them the day Steve and I drove over to the monastery not far from here. We had fun that day.

Sylvia is in a box on a plane right now. She's flying home to her family in a small village in Mexico where she'll be buried in a tiny graveyard full of flowers. If the Mexicans are right about what happens after you die, she's already in heaven. I hope they know what they're talking about for Sylvia's sake. Tomás, her husband, won't be attending the funeral. It's far too risky for Tomás to cross the border into Mexico. Who knows if he'd ever make it back? My dad talked to Tomás's employer, a factory farmer near here who plants genetically modified seeds from Monsanto. He grows corn, only corn, as far as the eye can see. He gets his laborers from a contractor who brings them in on horrible, crowded trucks like cattle. All of them, like Tomás and Sylvia, are part of an illegal workforce that people around here don't like to think about too much. They work cheap and they don't expect benefits. My dad asked the farmer if Tomás could have a few days off to deal with his affairs. Tomás is a good worker so he said he'll probably take him back but he couldn't promise anything. Why should his production suffer just because someone's wife died? he reasoned. Besides, according to his records, Tomás doesn't even exist. Rosa, the baby, is being sent to her grandparents in Mexico now because Tomás could never manage to take care of her if she stayed. He has no home here to speak of. Sylvia has a sister in the area, Wanda, but she's also a farm laborer with two kids back at home in Mexico. I'm not sure who's taking care of them but I sure hope someone is.

Sylvia was a housekeeper and a nanny for the Thompsons, who live in a development called Orchard Hill. It used to be a fruit orchard but pretty much all the trees had to be cut down to build the houses. There doesn't seem to be a hill anywhere either. When the accident happened, Sylvia had just dropped off two of the Thompson kids at a summer day camp and she was on her way home to clean the house before it was time to pick them up. People around here who knew her say she was a happy person and a good, honest worker. You would think that they'd be able to come up with something better than that. Does anyone really want to be remembered as a good, honest worker? I seriously doubt it. I'm sure she would prefer something like: *Sylvia loved to dance and had a wonderful singing voice. She loved her baby, Rosa, and hoped to send her to school in America one day. The smell of corn tortillas made her terribly homesick and the sound of mariachi music on the radio made her cry. She looked great in red and owned three red skirts. When she smiled at you her face lit up and it was impossible not to smile back.* Something like that.

From inside my darkroom I can hear Steve or Miguel

starting up the tractor, drowning out Bruce, our highly dys-functional rooster who crows almost all day long. He has a determined look on his face as though he's misplaced some-thing important like his keys, and he'll spend entire days scratching in the dry dirt looking for them. When he stops crowing for a while I find myself waiting for it. Aah, farm life.

My darkroom is an old supply shed, with blankets nailed over the windows, that my dad converted for me to fulfill a contractual agreement we arrived at on the day we left the Noe Valley house for good. He told me that if I let go of the banister and got in the car, he would build me a darkroom on the farm. Of course I needed that in writing. Parents are often full of empty promises when they want to motivate you and I needed a completion date for this alleged darkroom. I am, after all, the daughter of a lawyer. Before I got in the car I went up and down the street and delivered an index card with our new address and phone number to each of our neighbors just in case my mom came looking for us. They all looked at me like I was a sad orphan, which made me feel slightly better about the fact that I was get-ting away from this place where everyone knew at least part of my story.

My dad stuck to the contract. He insulated the shed and put in an old sink. He bought some used kitchen cabinets for storage and Formica countertops at a salvage yard to set a used Beseler enlarger on. It's pretty rustic but it's my first darkroom so I can't complain too much.

My dad has been on the phone all morning with the police and his lawyer friend Ned. He's hell-bent on making sure the woman who killed Sylvia (and walked away with a few scratches and a concussion) is charged. Miguel and Steve keep shaking their heads doubtfully. Steve told me that a rich white woman who hits an illegal Mexican immigrant with her car is likely never even going to hear about it again. If the roles were reversed, it would be a different story entirely. Sylvia would already be in prison. Well, my dad says that if the driver isn't charged he'll file a civil suit on behalf of her family, but Miguel isn't even hopeful about that. He says that the family won't want to stir up trouble and risk losing their jobs.

The Mexican people have a whole different take on death. They seem to view it as the other half of life. Not something to be feared. My favorite holiday when we lived in Noe Valley was the Day of the Dead, which happens every year right after Halloween. My mom and dad and I would walk down the hill to the Mission and buy sugar skulls at the bakery on Twenty-fourth Street and then we'd watch the parade of dancing skeletons and musicians and all sorts of ghoulish creatures go by. The idea is that the dead are gone but not forgotten. People wear pictures of their departed on a string around their necks and they build altars in their living rooms filled with candles and flowers and their dead relatives' favorite snack foods and drinks and cigarettes. It's a huge party with death as the theme. It's awfully cool. I've got a ton of pictures I've taken in a box somewhere.

When the photos dry I pull them off the clothesline and put them in a stack. I click off the red light and pull open the wooden door. Bright sunlight streams in and I squint like a hamster. Steve is transplanting arugula seedlings that were started in the greenhouse into one of our "small gardens." These are special raised gardens that are replanted all summer long so we always have fresh baby greens.

"Hey," I call out as I walk past him.

He lifts the wide brim of his straw sun hat. "Hey, Roar. Whatcha got there?"

"Photos of the accident for my dad."

"Lemme have a look." He stands up.

I walk over and hand him the stack. He takes them in his filthy hands and flips through them, shaking his head. He stops at the one of the overturned SUV.

"Hey, I know that SUV. That woman is *mucho* uptight. She went off on me the other day when I double-parked in front of Millie's for a nanosecond to deliver eggs."

"Yeah, we kind of got that impression too."

He hands the photos back to me. "Good CSI work, pal."

"Yeah, thanks. She probably won't even get charged." I squint up at him. Steve's about six feet tall.

"Nah, but what a load of bad karma."

"You believe in that stuff?" I ask.

"Sure. There's the criminal justice system, which isn't worth a hill of beans in this country unless you're white and rich, and then there's karmic justice, which is part of the natural order of the universe."

I nod. It makes sense to me. "Yeah. I suppose I believe in it too."

My mom was a believer. She always told me that bad karma catches up with you when you're least expecting it. She also told me that if you were cruel to animals you'd come back as one in your next life. I pointed out to her that Mittens, the cat who spent hours in her lap, could really be a bully who tied firecrackers to cats' tails. She thought about this and then she never said anything about it again. I felt like a real killjoy for stepping all over her theory.

Steve arches his back and bends over to touch his toes. I stand there feeling stupid. He straightens up again and takes off his hat and runs his fingers through his coarse wavy red hair. He puts his hat back on and looks over at the house.

"Tell your dad I'm going to need some help loading the truck for the market later."

"Okay."

"You gonna work it with me?" he asks.

"I dunno." I shrug like I don't care. My dad pays me eight bucks an hour to work the local farmers' market with Steve. What he doesn't know is that I would do it for free just to watch Steve charm all the local women. I love his easy way of talking to people, getting them to try new stuff, telling them how to cook the produce we sell. His passion for the food we grow makes the market fun.

"You know you want to." Steve grins and I practically have to turn away.

"You're right, Steve, I do. I live for it. When I was a little girl I used to say: 'One day I'd like to sell onions and garlic in the hot sun with Steve.'"

"Aw now, Miss Roar. I do believe you're messin' with me and that plain ain't nice."

I laugh. Steve's earnest farm-boy imitation always does me in.

I continue on up to the house with Rufus at my heels. I pull the screen door open and it wheezes shut behind me. My dad is at the kitchen table with a pad of paper and a pen. He's still on the phone. I can tell he doesn't like what he's hearing. He has deep furrows between his eyes. I put the photos on the table in front of him. He flips through them and stops at the one of Sylvia's foot.

"All right, look. I'll talk to her sister and I'll get back to you." He hangs up the phone.

"Steve needs help loading later."

"Where's Miguel?"

I shrug. "I dunno. Last time I saw him he was joyriding on the tractor."

My dad sighs. He's in no mood for my sarcasm. He continues to look at the photo. I fill a glass with cold water from the fridge.

"I guess we'd better get some apricots picked too. We lost a truckful on Tuesday. We'll have to try and make it back."

After the accident on Tuesday it was too late to get to the Ferry Plaza Farmers Market. We kept what we could for ourselves but we gave most of it away to the neighbors, and Miguel took some for his laborer friends who live in trailer camps called *colonias*, which is Spanish for over-crowded, hot, and inhumane.

"What are you up to, Roar?" asks my dad, pretending he's just curious.

"Storm's coming over," I say quickly. My dad makes a face. That's not the answer he was hoping for. I know he's about to ask a favor but we have a deal. He can play farmer if he wants but I'm not the "farmer's daughter." I do my chores but that's it.

"Hon, would you mind? I'd do it but I've got to track down Sylvia's sister."

I exhale heavily. "I'll do it but you need to know that I'm doing it for Sylvia." I put the empty glass down on the counter and head back outside. I try to slam the screen door behind me but the spring won't let me. It wheezes shut politely. I hear my dad yelling "Thank you!" but I'm already halfway to the orchard, taking long, angry, purposeful strides.

The first apricot I pluck off the tree smells of roses and sits heavy in my hand, warmed by the sun. I take a bite and savor the creamy, slightly tart taste that fills my mouth. I finish it in three bites, toss the pit, and get to some serious picking. Eventually Miguel joins me, his eyes crinkling up with good humor when he sees me scowling. He knows how things work around here and I can't help but laugh with him. The bees buzz lazily around a neat row of wooden hives next to the orchard. A local beekeeper leaves them here to pollinate our plants and we get a couple of free jars of honey out of it.

I hear Storm's scooter whining nasally up the road just as I'm loading the last box of apricots into the cool storage room. Rufus trots to the gate and escorts her in. Her pale arms and legs look out of place against the sunbaked dirt road where she parks her scooter. She waves and takes off her black helmet, hooking it over the handlebars. I walk toward her and she saunters past Steve, stopping for a brief flirtation, making sure he gets a good look at what she's not wearing. Her crotch-clearing skirt and tiny tank top leave very little to the imagination. Even from behind I can tell that Steve is being very good-natured about it.

Storm is the CEO in charge of making sure I acquire a misspent youth to regret when I'm older. My dad sent me to public school in the country and Storm is his punishment. She recently shaved off her eyebrows. She pencils them in now and always looks mildly surprised. The day I met her she walked over to me and said, "Aurora? Fabulous. I'm Storm. We're both forces of nature. Is there any doubt we were meant for each other?" That day her hair was hot pink and straightened into a pageboy. Right now it's black cherry and pulled back into a tight ponytail. I've also seen it silvery blond swept into a Marilyn Monroe style and royal blue shaved into a buzz cut. Her outfits are always outrageous too. They're the outfits you see in fashion magazines on nine-foot skeletal models. The ones where you always think, *Who would wear that?* Storm would, that's who.

Storm's parents are fundamentalist Christians, which involves a lot of Bible reading and praying and going to church. Storm (whose original name is Hillary) figured out pretty early in the game that when she rebels, her parents blame themselves. They put on hair shirts and wring their hands and ask God's forgiveness for the wrong turn they've taken in raising their only child. Then they pray for guidance. Storm keeps them on their toes by occasionally vomiting loudly with the bathroom door open after dinner so they can hear it at the dinner table or cutting herself in places on her body where they couldn't possibly miss it. She gets suspended from school regularly, and at our school, that's saying a lot. You practically have to run down the hallways waving a gun and screaming to get anyone's attention.

Storm's parents don't even think it's really her doing all this. They think it's Satan; very convenient for Storm, who counts Satan among her heroes. I try to warn her that an exorcism can't be far off.

"That's an attractive outfit," Storm says, taking in my too-big jeans cut off at the knee, gum boots, a ripped gray T-shirt, and a faded Metallica '95 summer tour baseball cap.

"You like it? It's right off the runway in Milan." I vogue for her.

"Your knee is bleeding," she says, unamused.

"I've gotta go put my suit on, you wanna come?"

"Nah, I don't like your dad's vibe. I'll wait here with Steve."

"I'll bet."

Up in my bedroom I pull my swimsuit on and put my clothes on over it.

Storm fires up the scooter and I jump on the back. We bump along on a potholed road that separates our farm from our neighbors, approaching top speeds of about fourteen miles an hour. I hang on to Storm's waist as she navigates around the holes. My camera bangs against my bony chest. We travel alongside cornfields and then a peach orchard and then a cherry orchard. It's the perfect picture of farm life. The type of thing you see in brochures where they try to coax city people to vacation on a "working farm."

We arrive at the swimming hole, a pretty pathetic "hole in the ground" type of thing. It sort of looks like the hole a meteor crashing to Earth might make but I'm sure the real story involves something that used to be there but isn't anymore. Those stories always make me sad. Hardly anyone comes here, and there's a rope swing hanging from a tree you can do the Tarzan thing on. Storm and I spread out our towels on a small patch of grass and pull off our clothes. We stretch out in the sun. Storm pulls out a pack of cigarettes from her embroidered bag and lights one like a movie star.

"Wanna ciggie?"

I shake my head. I like how she looks smoking but I think it's disgusting. Besides, I'm not part of the "youth in

revolt" movement she's heading up. With her cigarette bob-
bing in her lips and without sitting up, Storm pops open a
tube of SPF forty sunscreen and smears it all over herself. I
snap a couple of photos before she notices and starts posing.
I only take candids.

"So," she exhales, "I've been thinking you should tell
Steve that you want him to deflower you."

"Oh, okay, and how do you suppose talk would come
around to that?"

She shrugs. "That's up to you."

"Besides, he has a girlfriend."

Storm sits up on her elbows and looks over her femme
fatale sunglasses at me. "I don't see her anywhere near him,"
she says evenly.

Storm is on a campaign to end my virginity. She claims
that she lost hers last summer. She came home at about
eleven at night covered in hickies and loaded, walked into
the living room, where her parents were holding their
nightly prayer meeting, and announced that she'd just had
sex. Her mother crossed herself and looked to the ceiling. Her father sighed and left the room. So it's anybody's
guess whether it really happened or not. It could simply be
another vote for Satan. Who knows?

"Wanna swim?" asks Storm, still up on her elbows. She
puts out her cigarette in the sand.

"Sure." I jump to my feet and dash into the murky, cool

water with Storm at my heels. My bare feet sink into the mud and it oozes between my toes. Clouds of muddy water swirl around our thighs. When we're in up to our waists, we dive in and swim for the middle. It's deliciously chilly. We tread water facing each other for a minute and then Storm dives like a graceful duck into the murky abyss. I keep treading. The water smells briny.

Before Storm got wise to her parents they enrolled her in every available class they could find. Something about idle hands being the devil's workshop. Storm can swim like an Olympian, play piano and violin, tap-dance, give CPR, and throw pots. She was also a ballerina, a Girl Scout, and a prizewinning 4-H competitor all before she was twelve years old.

My parents sent me to Yoga For Kids! which was basically day care with yoga mats and some sort of visualization therapy that I bailed on after two classes. The rest of the time they encouraged me to take time to gaze at the clouds and look for truth in a blade of grass and generally explore my "feelings." Well, sometimes a cloud is just a cloud and a blade of grass is just a blade of grass and feelings are dangerous. Now I'm a mediocre swimmer and all I know on the piano is "Chopsticks." I also dance like a white girl but at least my mom taught me how to take a picture. At least there's that.

Before Storm surfaces, I notice someone sitting on the

banks behind some reeds, watching us. Storm's head pops up. Her black cherry hair has gone blue black. She looks like a seal.

"Hey, there's a perv over there watching us." I point.

Storm wipes the water out of her eyes and squints. "That's not a perv, that's Forest."

"Forest who? Gump?"

"Forest Gilwood."

"Gilwood? The kid whose mom killed Sylvia?"

"Yeah. He's here for the summer. His dad lives in L.A."

"I saw him at the hospital that day. Who was the creep he was with?"

"That was probably his stepdad, Mega-creep."

Forest isn't watching us anymore. His head is bent over a notebook in his lap and he's writing.

"What's he like?" I ask, watching him as I bob in the water.

"I dunno, kind of quiet, I guess. He mostly keeps to himself."

"Wow, what must it be like to be that woman's kid?"

"Yeah, I'm sure it's a real treat."

"So how do you know him?"

"Honey, I know everyone." She winks at me and starts swimming for the shore.

4

The next place I see him is at the local farmers' market on Saturday. I'm dragging a box of apricots out of the back of the pickup and thinking about a dream I had the night before about Sylvia's foot. In the dream, her disembodied foot had little wings attached to it just like in the paintings my mom used to paint. The foot was flying in a zigzag pattern like a bird, higher and higher, while I stood on the ground with my head bent back, watching it. Suddenly I was aware of a dark, shadowy faceless figure standing next to me. He was watching the foot through the sights of a rifle with one eye squeezed shut and then *blam*! He shot at it as though it were a clay pigeon. He missed completely and I watched the foot flap its wings and disappear into the clouds. I looked around but the gunman had disappeared too.

I spot Forest across the plaza, wandering through the

market aimlessly, which is odd. Most people come here with a purpose. He looks completely disinterested in all things produce-related. He has a weathered canvas book bag slung across his shoulder that sets him apart from anyone else around here. The hippie organic farmers would embrace it as a cool accessory but the redneck farmers would call it a purse. I'm pretty confident that the pad he was scribbling on at the swimming hole is in that bag somewhere. I grab my camera and snap a stealth photo. Steve looks up at me for a second but I've already put my camera down.

I keep one eye on Forest as I work the stall, making change, weighing bags of produce, giving out samples. Our farm is called The Good Earth and we're a very popular stall because we sell a big variety of things. People around here know that we're not USDA certified organic but we don't use any pesticides or herbicides. My dad refused to "jump through the United States Department of Agriculture's hoops" (as he so delicately put it) to get certified so he's now known as something of an anarchist farmer. Fortunately he has a face you can trust with your life, and when Steve is back at school and he works this market himself, he preaches the good word about our food to anyone within hearing range. He's accumulated quite a devoted following. Plus, when he's not here we have Steve, and no one can resist Steve.

When you work a stall at the market, you pick up the news of the week in snippets. You don't have to participate; you don't even have to make eye contact. It just comes at you. But today the news is all about "the accident." Everyone knows I was there so I get a lot of people asking me what I saw. I don't really want to talk about it. I shrug. They shake their heads sympathetically. I keep my head down and I hear what they're saying: *That's the girl, she was there; poor thing. Did you hear? The Thompsons' nanny was killed; what was her name again? I don't remember, she was Mexican . . . illegal; the Thompsons are devastated, the kids adored her; I heard Connie Gilwood was in a terrible accident, you know her, Jerry's wife? He sold us our first house. The one with the columns and the pool; is she okay? I hear she had a concussion; the SUV was totaled; that road is so dangerous.*

Forest makes his way over to us, one stall at a time. He stops at the Goat's Milk Soap stall near us and smells a few bars. When he lifts his eyes to talk to the soap maker I can see, even from here, that they are sea-glass green. My pulse quickens and I think I feel the Earth move slightly.

Steve is singing the praises of green garlic to a woman in a big sun hat who's never heard of it. He's practically telling her it will cure cancer. She buys two bunches and he tells her with a wink she'll be back next week for more. I'm pretty sure she will. I hand a bag of the first zucchini of the season to a woman and count out her change. Out of the corner of my eye I can see Forest approaching. I'm not sure he'll remember me, but when our eyes meet I see a light go on.

"Hi," he says. His eyes dart quickly around and I realize that his mom, or maybe even his stepdad, must be somewhere in the crowd.

I smile and offer him an apricot. He smells it and then drops it into his book bag.

"Not in there, it'll get smooshed."

He digs around and retrieves it but he holds it awkwardly in his hand.

"Eat it," I encourage him. "It's food. Surely they have it on your planet?" I weigh a bag of fava beans and take three dollars from a woman.

He looks extremely uncomfortable. "Hey, um. I know this is weird but I wanted to tell you how sorry I am about that woman." He's still holding the apricot in midair.

"Sylvia. Her name was Sylvia."

"Right. Sylvia. I know you were there and I'm sorry about it all." He lets the hand with the apricot drop to his side.

"Sure." I feel a pang of guilt. My dad would flip if he saw me fraternizing with the enemy, let alone flirting, if that's what I'm doing. I don't know what's wrong with me but I can't help myself. I wish my hair wasn't tied back with a rubber band meant for bunching asparagus. I wish I wasn't wearing my dad's shirt. I wish I'd at least bothered with mascara. I look every bit the person I've been trying to avoid for two years. I look like a farmer's daughter. I could die. Steve glances over at me and I give him a "don't tell my dad" look. One he's all too familiar with. He nods quickly.

I change the subject. "Hey, was that you at the swimming hole yesterday?" I immediately regret using the phrase "swimming hole." That's hardly what it is and I sound like a total local yokel. I may as well be wearing overalls and pigtails and sporting a blacked-out front tooth.

"Yeah. I saw you there too. I hope I didn't creep you out. I wanted to let you know I was there but then it was too late."

I shrug. "No, it was cool. You didn't have to leave."

He smiles a little and then he just stares at me. I brush my hand over my face quickly. It's entirely possible that I have food lodged somewhere.

"What?" I'm desperate to know what he's staring at.

"Oh, um, nothing. I was just looking at your eyes. They just turned the most amazing shade of blue." He blushes.

My eyes change color? I'm quite certain that they don't, and while we're on the topic of amazing eyes? *Right back at ya, buddy.* Out loud I say, "Thanks."

"Oh, honey, there you are! I've been looking everywhere for you!" Suddenly his mother appears out of nowhere, her torpedo boobs leading the way. Forest's sea-glass eyes narrow slightly. Our moment is abruptly over. He moves away from our stall with a nervous glance in my direction. Steve is watching us and he puts two and two together. His gentle face clouds over.

"Man, someone's got a lotta nerve coming around here."

Forest's mom seems to have made a speedy recovery. She has a tiny bandage above her perfectly shaped right eyebrow, and one of her eyes is a little purple underneath but she's got so much makeup on it that you can barely notice it. In fact her whole face looks fresh from a cosmetics counter makeover. Her eye shadow perfectly matches her aqua velour tracksuit. The effect is a sort of desperate Heather Locklear look. Seeing her, I feel rage rising up in me, like I could close my hands around her throat and squeeze until she stops breathing. She hustles Forest away. He's still holding the apricot in his right hand. I feel cheated. I crave more of him. After they disappear into the crowd I have to wonder what Connie Gilwood would want with a farmers' market when she seems hell-bent on trying to kill every farmer she comes in contact with.

Steve and I get seriously caught up in the business of selling vegetables because as the two p.m. closing time approaches, every pound we sell is a pound we don't have to load back on the truck. We end up having a good day, selling out of almost everything, which hardly ever happens.

On the drive home Steve starts firing off questions at me about Forest. He wants to know "what's up with that guy," in a protective big brother sort of way.

"Nothing," I say. And that's the truth. There's nothing to tell. Steve's got some crappy noisy garage band CD playing on the stereo. These days it just seems way too easy for anyone out there with a guitar to make a CD. I tolerated it on the way to the market but now I'm tired and dirty and hating myself for not wearing mascara and hating myself more for caring about mascara. I'm also, for the first time ever, thinking that eight dollars an hour doesn't seem like nearly enough for what I do.

"Hey, can we take this crap off? It's giving me a headache."

"C'mon, Roar, it's great."

I press the eject button on the stereo and when the CD slides out I grab it and hold it out my open window.

"I'm dropping it."

"Don't, Roar, it's my only copy."

With my free hand I flip through my dad's CD case on the seat between us.

"Bob Dylan?" I ask.

Steve sighs. "Which one?"

"*Nashville Skyline* or *Blood on the Tracks*."

"*Blood on the Tracks*."

I pull his crappy CD back into the cab and put it on the seat. I take the Dylan CD out of my dad's case and put it into the player. Steve grins at me.

"Well, aren't we in a mood today."

I pull the rubber asparagus band out of my tangled hair and hang my head out the open window, letting the wind take hold of it.

When we arrive back at the farm, my dad, the farmer, actually appears to be doing farmwork. He and Miguel are out in the field working on a fallen fence. Steve goes out to join them. In a couple of hours he'll head to Berkeley to visit Jane. He's off on Sundays and he usually spends them with her.

I walk heavily up the stairs to my bedroom and pull off my dirty clothes, leaving them in a heap on the floor. Rufus joins me, curling up on the rag rug next to my bed. I slide between the cool sheets and think about Forest. He wanted me to know that he was sorry about Sylvia. What does that mean? Does it mean that he wants me to know that he understands that what his mom did was horrible? I'm pretty sure that the story she must have told him isn't the whole truth, but by now he must have heard several versions of it. There isn't anyone in a fifty-mile radius of this place who doesn't know a version of it. He's probably drawn his own conclusions. I think about this until I eventually drift off to sleep.

I wake to the sound of my dad speaking Spanish on the phone downstairs in the kitchen. I look at my bedside clock. I've been asleep for a little over an hour. From what little Spanish I know, I figure out that he's talking to Sylvia's sister, Wanda. His tone goes from hushed to insistent and back to hushed. He says good-bye to her the way you do when the person on the other end suddenly has to hang up because someone walked into the room who isn't supposed to hear. I know that my dad's not done with her, though.

When I appear in the doorway of the kitchen he smiles at me strangely.

"What?"

"You look more like your mother every day." He looks at me with a combination of sadness and pride.

"I do?" I ask, as though I don't already know this. I have her thick black hair and her blue eyes and even her lips. I see her in my face every time I look in the mirror.

"How'd the market go?"

"Good." I scratch my head and yawn. "Didn't Steve tell you?" I pull the lemonade out of the fridge.

"Yeah. I guess." He looks distracted. "Hey, I was just talking to Sylvia's sister, Wanda, and I think I'm going to give Sylvia's husband, Tomás, a job here on the farm. Steve's back at school in September and I think we've got enough work for an extra man year-round now."

I shrug. "Sure, okay." I hardly give it a thought, but then it occurs to me that if Tomás is actually here working on the property it would be easier for my dad to badger him into filing a civil suit against Connie Gilwood. Hmm. I smell a rat.

"Hey, it's just about the work, right? You're not going to get all lawyery on him, are you?"

"Nah, not at all. I just think he'll be happier here and I'll pay him what he's worth. It's the right thing to do." He looks away as he says this.

I think about Forest and I feel my own pang of guilt. I take my lemonade out to the back porch and sit in the rocker. The sun is dipping low in the sky and a soft cool breeze has just come up, ruffling the leaves on the big oak above me. Steve drives by in his Jeep on his way to Berkeley. He toots his horn and waves. He holds up a CD for me to see, the crappy garage band CD, I assume. He grins mischievously. I glare at him and he blows me a kiss. He looks like a guy who's about to have a lot of sex. Rufus escorts him to the gate and then trots back to the porch, where he lays down with a sigh at my feet.

5

*S*torm dips a fry into a puddle of ketchup that almost exactly matches the open-wound shade of her long fingernails. The sun through the diner window bounces off a ruby ring on her middle finger the size of the Hope Diamond. It's a family heirloom. Her great-great-grandmother brought it over from the old country (is there really just one "old country"?). Storm stole it from her mother's jewelry box this morning. She wears the key to that box on a silver chain around her neck. She had it copied at the hardware store several months ago and then she put the original back in its hiding spot under her mom's modest collection of lingerie. Now she has free access to the family jewels, which, she maintains, is her birthright.

My own fingernails, I notice, as I cut into a grilled cheese sandwich, are raggedly cut with overgrown cuticles and dirt underneath them. I try to remember the exact moment I stopped caring about them. The truth is, I never cared about them like Storm cares about hers. My mom and I used to paint our fingernails together but we could never seem to stick with one color and we ended up with hands that looked like a box of crayons. Storm's fingernails are sharpened into perfect points that she uses to punctuate her sentences. They're like her exclamation marks.

I'm telling her about my encounter with Forest.

"Listen, Roar, we don't live in Manhattan. There aren't a thousand Starbucks, a million gyms, and a dry cleaner on every corner. We don't go 'clubbing' all the time." She punctuates "clubbing" with finger quotes.

I don't bother telling her that even if we did live in Manhattan, I wouldn't be caught dead in any of those places.

"So, what's your point?"

"I'm getting to it. There's dick-all to do around here, okay?" She tabulates our town out on her fingers. "There are three restaurants, one of them serves edible food and you're looking at it. There's a post office, a hardware store, a library, a grocery store, a beauty salon, a gas station, a car dealership, a feed store, and . . ." Storm starts a staring contest with a little girl dressed in her Sunday best sitting with her family in the booth across from us. The little girl loses. Her curiosity may have been piqued by Storm's Sunday best: a pair of striped kneesocks that stop at midthigh, a thrift-store sequined mini in pale blue, cut off unevenly with a pair of scissors, and four-inch platform sandals. Her hair is pulled back into a single braid and her mouth is a slash of deep red. She's wearing colored contact lenses that make her eyes look lavender like Elizabeth Taylor's.

". . . don't forget Red's Recovery Room," I add. Red's is our infamous town bar, especially popular on Thursdays for karaoke night.

"Right. And you're surprised that he turned up at the farmers' market? It's the social event of the week around here. It's not like your planets aligned or something." She waves a fry matter-of-factly, dashing any hopes I may have that Forest may actually have been looking for me. I'm not sure I understand why she won't give me this; I mean, would it kill her? She leans back, satisfied. "That's my point."

Millie stops by our booth with a fresh pot of coffee and fills our cups. Millie's diner used to be the busiest place around for Sunday brunch. She uses fresh local ingredients that she buys directly from the farmers. She often buys eggs and seasonal vegetables from us. She used to run a farm with her husband till the marriage went up in smoke. She moved into town and started the diner. The farmer she used to be still lingers on her face. Her skin is tan and her cheeks are ruddy. She has strong sinewy arms and a wide, easy smile. She's the real deal. Her diner is an extension of her personality. I like the bottles of real maple syrup on the tables and the little cow-shaped pitchers of cream for the coffee. The place reminds me of a diner out of a fifties movie where everyone is deliriously happy and oblivious to the real world. There's even an old jukebox with the original vinyl 45's in it. About a year ago, they built a Denny's about five miles away in a brand-new strip mall off the interstate and a lot of the after-church crowd started going over there for Grand Slam breakfasts. Millie still gets her fair share of the locals, though, and now she has more time to get out of the kitchen and talk to customers.

"Damn shame about Sylvia," she says, shaking her head. "How's your dad, Roar?"

"He's okay. He's trying to help out with her family, maybe get a lawsuit together."

Millie looks around quickly. "Some folks around here have been saying that your dad's stirring up a hornet's nest, but I say we should do right by those people. A woman is dead, a mother no less. Why should it make a difference if she's legal or not?" She puts a hand on her hip and juts out her chin. I automatically move my hand to my camera on the seat next to me but I know that Millie would never stand for a photo. Whenever I see a face that moves me, I go for the camera; it's like I've got an itchy trigger finger.

The little girl's father lowers his menu and watches us.

I know him. Everyone does. He's the ne'er-do-well son of the biggest landowner in the county, Samuel Burk. His name is Brody. His dad used to run cattle but he recently got tired of it. He somehow got his land rezoned, sold off all the livestock, and now Brody is selling the land off like pieces of a patchwork quilt for development into crappy tract homes. He ran for congressman of our district in the last election and lost. He's still smarting from that. My dad calls him "Big Hat, No Cattle" in reference to the black cowboy hat Brody wears around town. He's anti-farm, pro-development, and he's very vocal about his wish to run every migrant farmworker out of here. When the ranch was still running, Brody's dad, Sam, was forced to hire Mexican ranch hands. Ranch work had lost its appeal to the kids growing up around here. Brody was still working for his dad even though it's rumored that they never got along. Apparently, Sam used to get blind drunk and knock the crap out of Brody. He ended up in the hospital with a broken collarbone once after Sam threw him down a flight of stairs. Brody took it out on the Mexicans. He refused to learn any Spanish; he taunted them and called them stupid. There was a rumor floating around here that he and his "good ol' boy" idiot friends got drunk and took a couple of Mexican ranch hands out in his truck, allegedly to work on some water wells. The Mexicans were never heard from again.

No one looked for them very hard. Mexicans disappear from around here all the time, and since they don't technically exist, no one cares too much.

I look right through Brody and he raises his menu again. His long-suffering wife, a former beauty queen who won Miss Something Or Other a decade ago, blots at a puddle of soda with a stack of napkins. The kid who created it, one of a set of twins, dumps more soda on the table and watches his mom defiantly while the other twin laughs.

Two Hispanic men sitting on stools at the counter look over their shoulders at us and exchange glances with the short-order cook, Juan, who's from El Salvador. Millie is oblivious. When you're in her diner, you're in her country and she says what she thinks.

"Can I get you girls anything else?" she asks.

"Nah. Just the bill." I smile at her.

"You say hi to your dad for me, okay?" she says, dropping the bill on the table.

"I will, Millie, thanks."

Just as I'm digging around in the pocket of my jeans for my half of the bill, the bell on the front door of the diner tinkles and Storm looks up, amused.

"Well, it looks like your boyfriend found the only edible food in town." She looks smug. Her point has been made.

I look over my shoulder. Forest makes his way over to

a stool at the counter and orders a coffee to go from Millie. He makes eye contact with Storm and nods. When he sees me, he gets up off the stool and walks over to our booth. His book bag is on his shoulder and he's wearing the Misfits T-shirt again. Millie watches all this with some interest as she puts his coffee near the register and wipes down the counters.

Now he's standing in front of our booth looking slightly uncomfortable.

"Hey," he says.

"Hey," we both say. I scramble for topics.

Storm, a conversational magician, jumps in. "I was just telling Roar here how you're from L.A. How do you like country life?"

He shrugs. "It's pretty minimal but it's okay, I guess. The open space is good for the head."

It appears I've become mute. I rifle through my brain files for L.A. stories. The only one I come up with is the time I threw up on my shoes at Disneyland. No, that's no good.

"Yeah, I suppose," says Storm, nudging me with her platform sandal. "I guess I know what you mean, but then I always say it's a nice place to visit but you wouldn't want to live here."

Forest stuffs his hands into the front pockets of his

jeans and laughs. He glances at me. I offer up a thin smile. God, I wish I had some fruit to give him. I'm so much better at this when I'm standing behind a bunch of zucchini. It gives me a purpose, something to do with my hands, which are now nervously playing with my hair.

"Well, you must miss your girlfriend. You do have a girlfriend, don't you?" asks Storm.

"No." One hand comes out of a pocket and scratches his head.

I kick Storm in the shin. She glares at me, her eyes wide.

Forest nods toward my camera. "What have you got there, a Nikon?"

"Yeah. An FM."

"Cool. What do you shoot? Color or black-and-white?"

"Mostly black-and-white, a bit of color."

"May I?" He picks up my camera off the seat.

"Be my guest."

"Digital?"

"Nah, I'm old-school." Now we're getting somewhere.

"Where do you get it processed?"

"I mostly do my own. I have a darkroom. Some of it I take to the Looking Glass in Berkeley." The truth is I give it to Steve to drop off for me.

The look on his face tells me that I might be racking up some cool points with him. He looks through the viewfinder at me and adjusts the focus. He snaps a photo before I have a chance to make my camera face.

"Nice picture," he says, laying the camera down carefully. "Well, my coffee's ready. I'll see you around, I guess."

I grope for meaning in his last words but maybe he just meant "I'll see you around." Around where? The barn dance? The book club? The Old Timer's Cookout? Target practice? He strolls over to the register and pays Millie for the coffee. The bell tinkles again and he's gone, walking up the street the way he came. I crane my neck and watch him out the glass window till he disappears.

"Okay, you really suck at talking to guys," says Storm, disgusted.

"I know, I know. I never said I was any good at it."

She shrugs. "Well, he's weird anyway. He likes you, though."

"How can you tell?"

"It was pretty obvious. Man, Roar, sometimes it's really hard to believe you're a city girl."

On the way home, riding behind Storm on her scooter, her little skirt flapping in the breeze for everyone driving by to get a good look at her underwear (and by "everyone" I mean four cars), I muse over Forest. How do you figure out a guy like that? Most of the people around here can be sorted into nice tidy categories just by observing a few clues. If a guy drives a truck with nine-foot wheels and a rifle rack, well, I think you can pretty much figure out how he voted in the last election and you could probably even go so far as to say that he doesn't support feminism. If a person is driving a truck that runs on biodiesel with a Grateful Dead bumper sticker and he or she is wearing Birkenstocks, it's not too hard to fill in the rest. But Forest? He's a tough one. He's not giving me too many clues, and if Storm is right and he likes me, he's playing it pretty cool.

Storm drops me at my mailbox and I walk up the road toward the house. I'm wondering where Rufus got to until I see a familiar truck parked next to my dad's. It belongs to Reynaldo Valdez. He's a grape grower from the next county over and a good friend of my dad's. Rufus loves Reynaldo more than life itself, which makes me think that he's a very good judge of character. When Reynaldo visits, no one else exists for Rufus; a gang of wandering thieves could rob us blind and Rufus would just sit there licking Reynaldo's hand.

Reynaldo came to California from Mexico at sixteen and lied about his age to get a job in the vineyards. He has a third-grade education but he worked really hard. He rode a bike he bought for twenty dollars to the vineyard every day. Now he manages nine hundred acres of wine grapes in two counties. In the last few years, he started bottling wine under the Valdez name. His success story is rare, though. Reynaldo has been a U.S. citizen since 1996 but most of the Latinos who come to California from Mexico to work the vineyards are undocumented and most of them won't ever be citizens. My dad goes on and on about how congress wants to spend billions to keep these people out. The California wine industry would be crippled without them. Not to mention the agriculture industry. Reynaldo met my dad back when we lived in the city. My dad defended his nephew, who'd been charged with jacking a car in the Presidio. His nephew was in Sacramento at the time of the carjacking. It was a clear case of mistaken identity. Reynaldo and my dad got on like a house on fire and they've been good friends ever since.

I pick up my pace and skip up the wooden porch steps and into the house. Reynaldo is sitting at the table with my dad. They each have a glass of red wine in front of them, and a dusty bottle sits in the middle of the table next to Reynaldo's signature straw cowboy hat. When Reynaldo sees me, he jumps from his chair and gives me a bear hug.

"Aurora borealis! Let me look at you!" he says in his thickly accented English. He stands back and holds my hand up in the air, spinning me around as though we're dancing. "*Hermosa*, beautiful! Senorita, if I were a young man I would run off with you!"

"Stop it, Reynaldo." I giggle. He's been promising to run away with me since I was six. His charm always melts me into a puddle. He has the kind of face you could look at for hours: darkly handsome with intense laughing eyes, broad cheekbones, and dazzling white teeth. I know that he wants to tell me that I look like my mother, who adored him, but he knows better than to say that in front of my dad. Rufus hangs on his every word and tries to situate himself as close as possible to Reynaldo without actually getting in his lap. Reynaldo sits back down in his chair and absentmindedly scratches Rufus's head.

"Aurora, try our new cabernet."

He hands me his glass and I take a sip. The deep, woody scent travels up my nose. It tastes rich and grapey and old. It makes me think of cool dark rooms made of oak.

"Delicious." I smack my lips. "The best so far."

He beams. "We produced only one hundred cases and all of them are spoken for already," he says proudly.

My dad leans back in his chair. He sips his wine and grins. He's watched Reynaldo struggle for so many years and it does him good to see Reynaldo happy and successful. We haven't seen Reynaldo out here for some time; it's a long drive over here from where he lives, and I have a feeling he might be here to talk to my dad about the Sylvia matter. My dad respects his opinion and he knows only too well what

Reynaldo's dealt with since he left Mexico.

I leave them alone. I have some film to develop out in my darkroom. Even as I head out the back door, I can hear their voices becoming louder and angrier as they switch back and forth from Spanish to English. I know that this argument will go on for some time and end in hugs and maybe even some tears. I've seen it before. Otherwise, the farm is quiet. Bruce crows from time to time, breaking the silence, but Sunday is a day off for Miguel and Steve and it's the most peaceful day of the week around here. The crickets fill the air with a soft electric buzz. Even the neat rows of vegetables seem to be relaxing, basking in the bright sunlight, their leaves ruffling slightly in the gentle breeze off the delta. The air is perfumed with dill and lavender. I wander over to the Mission fig trees, letting my feet drag in the dirt, kicking up the dust. I pluck a couple of perfect purple orbs. I tear one of them open and study its crimson jeweled interior before I take a bite. It tastes like a faraway place to me.

6

$\mathcal{T}$he first time I saw the farm it was hard to hide my disappointment. Even though I must have had a rough idea of what a farm out here might look like, I'd somehow built a fantasy farm in my mind with pretty wooden fences and sleek horses with billowing manes and tails prancing around their paddocks. I'd pictured a butter yellow farmhouse with white trim and neatly painted outbuildings to match, and an archway over the drive with "Lazy K" written on it and a horseshoe for luck. I suppose I'd probably read too many Pony Club Camp books as a kid. The fantasy farm probably exists in Kentucky somewhere but it has nothing to do with the farm my dad bought.

The first thing I noticed when we pulled into the driveway was a tornado of dust swirling around in front of the car and I thought, *Great, a twister. Grab Toto.* I had no idea that it was a sign of things to come. Dust coats everything on a farm: the buildings, your car, your skin, your hair, and even your teeth.

I looked at my dad with what must have been alarm but he was already out of the car, excited to show me "the place."

The farmhouse looked abandoned, not the kind of abandoned where the windows are boarded up but recently abandoned, and badly in need of a coat of paint. In fact, the entire farm was in need of a coat of paint. Every piece of wood on every building screamed "I'm old and I'm tired." Rusted out pieces of farm equipment were scattered everywhere and had been there so long that monster weeds were growing up around them. An old truck with no wheels or windows or doors sat next to an outbuilding with springs escaping from the cracked leather on the seats.

Bob Soames, the farmer who my dad bought the farm from, had left the day before. He moved, with his wife, to a retirement community in Phoenix with a nine-hole golf course and an Olympic-size pool featuring Aquacise classes. They don't allow pets there, at least not mangy farm dogs, so Rufus was the only member of our welcoming committee. He seemed awfully happy to see us and I can't imagine how traumatizing it must have been for him to watch a moving van full of furniture pull away without being asked to come along. Did he just sit there on the porch all night long, hoping they would come back? We bonded right away, my first farm friend and I.

My dad chose this farm because Farmer Bob was deep into organic farming. The soil was already in good shape and he wouldn't have to detox the place. He could start farming organically immediately. In other words, he bought this place based on a pile of dirt. Pretty farmhouses didn't figure into the equation; in fact, I wouldn't be surprised if my dad hadn't even looked at the house.

We walked through the property with Rufus in the lead. My dad kept trying to make me visualize how it was all going to look when he was finished with it but it only made me tired. I just couldn't imagine how we could possibly do it all, but my dad was full of energy and ideas and he almost skipped from place to place, talking, planning, and quoting from his sustainable farming books till my head hurt. He seemed to have it all figured out but I was doubtful. I couldn't recall my dad ever completing even a simple home-improvement project when we lived in the city, and just because you wake up one morning and start calling yourself a farmer, that doesn't mean you are one.

After we walked the property we went back up to the house and pulled open the creaky screen door. The house smelled a bit like rotting wood. Bob had left some furniture behind; basically, all the stuff that didn't belong in his shiny new life: a La-Z-Boy recliner with worn-out armrests in the living room, a wooden rocker, and a radio the size of a Buick that looked like it was about a hundred years old (my dad was quick to let me know it worked). In the kitchen they left us an old farm table and six mismatched chairs. The cupboards were empty but the pantry held jars of pickles and jams and tomatoes, all carefully labeled and dated in small, precise handwriting.

I went upstairs to my new bedroom and sat on the edge of the iron bed frame. Without a mattress it looked like a medieval torture device. I looked around at the faded rose wallpaper and felt like I was a thousand miles from anything meaningful. Instead of getting ourselves a new life, we'd taken over someone else's old discarded life. I couldn't imagine how I would survive in this place. I looked up at the stained, cracked ceiling and vowed that I would find a way out somehow.

My dad hired Javier, an odd-job carpenter and the brother of Jesus, the plumber. Javier arrived very early every morning and set to work with my dad on his list of jobs.

The first job on the list was the bunkhouse, a place for the farmworkers to sleep. Dad chose a storage shed for this and Javier patched the roof and insulated the walls and then nailed sheets of plywood over the insulation. I painted the plywood white, first painting six-foot curse words and then painting white over them. If Javier saw them he never said anything. My dad bought two sets of bunk beds from a now-defunct Christian summer camp and we wrestled them through the door. The final touch on the bunkhouse was an outdoor shower. It ended up looking pretty rustic, but then we weren't exactly building the Four Seasons Hotel. The outhouse was already there but my dad and Javier "upgraded" it, which means they put a new toilet seat on and fixed the door so you could lock it.

As soon as the bunkhouse was done my dad hired Steve and Miguel so that we could start the business of farming immediately. He found Steve at a farmers' market in Berkeley and they hit it off right away. He offered him better money than he was making and the position of farm manager. Miguel appeared at our door one morning and my dad hired him on the spot after looking at his calloused hands. Farmer Bob had done a fine job of getting a lot of stuff in the ground before he left (he must have known our first year would be a struggle). All we had to do was water and feed it and let it do its thing. It would be our meager income for the coming months till we got the farm up and running. My dad sweet-talked his way into the Ferry Plaza Farmers Market in San Francisco, and getting a stall at the Saturday market here in town was a breeze. Then he started working on local and not-so-local restaurants, promising fresh produce deliveries twice a week. We were the first farm from out here to do that and a lot of chefs were eager to give it a try.

When Javier and my dad finished my darkroom, they moved on to a farm stand on the roadside next to the farm's gate. It's sort of like a grown-up version of a lemonade stand. These farm stands are everywhere out here and they work on the honor system. You take what you want and leave the money in a coffee can. Even the Buddhist monastery up the road has one. They sell perfect fragrant ambrosia melons and an odd assortment of exotic Asian produce.

Now, being a city girl, I assumed that the coffee can would disappear in a hot minute, but it didn't. In fact, I've never heard of anyone's coffee can disappearing. It's like the coffee cans are considered sacred. Stealing one would be like taking one of those collection boxes next to the candles in a church. You would surely get hit by a bolt of lightning on your way out. Besides, here in farm country people don't like to mess with one another's livelihoods.

Somehow (because no one else would do it), it became my job to stock the farm stand and collect the money every day. Whatever we were selling had to be weighed out into little green baskets that held roughly a pound, or else I would have to bunch lavender and rosemary into neat bouquets with a rubber band, which left a scent on my fingers that would last for days. Then I would post the prices on a little chalkboard.

I often pointed out to my dad that, before we moved here, I didn't have a job, nor did I want one, and suddenly I seemed to be working ten hours a day on something that I had absolutely no interest in. He was always quick to respond with the fact that the alternative was school. I'd wrapped up ninth grade at my city school early after my dad spoke with my teachers and arranged for me to take all my exams before we left. It didn't hurt that my grades were already good. My grades have somehow always been good. I even skipped sixth grade (a curse back then; I still looked like a little girl among all the developing "young women"). If I'd known that my dad was arranging for all this so that he'd have slave labor, I probably wouldn't have been so excited about finishing school early. School was never this hard. At night, my dad and I fell into bed exhausted. I'd never been so tired in my life, and a day on a farm starts alarmingly early, so something as luxurious as sleeping in is out of the question. My pale Irish skin had developed little freckles everywhere even with goo-gobs of sunscreen, and I was covered in scrapes and cuts and bruises.

Steve and Miguel got to work putting in raised beds with drip irrigation. We would be growing all things green in these: baby spinach, arugula, pepper cress, and mache. After they finished that, they cleaned out the greenhouse, chased away the pigeons, and replaced the broken glass panes. This is where we would start the seeds for the baby greens and most of the other plants and then transplant them to the raised beds and the regular garden. My dad and Steve also planted a few marijuana plants in there for their "private use" and tended them like they were premature newborns in an incubator.

It took me a solid week to clean out the ancient barn. I hauled out enough crap to make a giant bonfire. You could probably see it from space. I was stung by two bees on two separate days and then I cut my knuckle open on a glass window. Who knew there was so much blood in a knuckle? I lost about a gallon of it before my dad and Steve got me to the hospital. I looked like the star of a slasher movie. I also threw up in the hospital parking lot. Not pretty.

There are three stalls in the barn from back when they kept horses. With a shovel and a wheelbarrow I cleared out all the straw and the thousand-year-old poop. I came across a bat and her tiny baby bats, sleeping upside down with their leathery wings wrapped around them like Dracula's cape. Under the straw in one of the stalls, I found a bunch of loose boards, which I pried up, hoping for a hidden treasure: a chest of gold coins or bullion or bonds or

71

anything to help get me out of this mess. Instead I found a black metal box and a rat trap with a dried-up rat in it. The box was filled with old photos: several sepia-toned wedding photos of a handsome, young, large-eared groom and his delicate-looking bride. They appear shy and hopeful. There was another photo of the groom but in this one he's in an army uniform. He looks proud and scared at the same time. There was also one of a baby in a christening gown, a beautiful little girl with rosebud lips. The last photo in the stack was our farmhouse, newly painted with window boxes and a porch swing. A little girl in a smocked dress and white patent leather shoes is sitting on the porch steps. The oak tree barely touches the top of the eaves and there's a rooster weather vane on the spine of the roof. I figured that this must be the first young family to own this place and I wondered what happened to them. I wondered if they were able to make a go of things here or if the husband even made it back from the war. In the box I also found a Saint Christopher medallion on a chain and an army medal, a bronze cross with an outstretched hawk or an eagle in the middle. I couldn't imagine why anyone would leave these mementos behind. How could a person forget about them? I took the box into the house and put it in my dresser drawer.

My dad and I made a lot of trips into town for food and supplies. While my dad went over to the bank or the post office, I would go to the grocery store. People in town all seemed to know who I was: "the daughter of that fella who took over the Soameses' place." I guess the fact that we were driving his old truck gave us away. They all wanted to know what we had planned for the place and they wished us lots of luck. The grocer always threw something extra in my bag for me like a licorice whip or some bubble gum, like I was seven years old.

The other thing about farm life that they don't tell you is that the work is never done. A person could go insane, running around fixing things and doing chores only to start all over again every morning. But after we got through a lot of my dad's list, things didn't seem quite so urgent. We were selling the produce, money was starting to trickle in, and most of the farm was in decent shape. Don't get me wrong, if you wandered onto our property, the first thought that would come to you would be *wow, what a dump*, but to us it was a vast improvement.

I finally got to take a little time for myself and I walked out to the back pasture, which isn't a pasture anymore because Farmer Bob never had any grazing animals and neither do we. Rufus was taking one of his famous naps on the rag rug under the kitchen table so I grabbed my camera and ventured out alone. The grasses were thigh high and I had to push them aside as I made my way toward a stand of trees in the middle of the pasture that I'd always been curi-ous about. Why would a farmer clear a big field of trees and leave a stand of them like that? My first thought, of course, was that it was for sacrificing virgins at midnight. I could have sworn I'd heard moaning coming from that direction when I got up to use the bathroom in the middle of the night.

When I finally came upon the stand it was much larger than I'd imagined it, a mini forest surrounded by an entire field of grasses. The trees were old and gnarled and the air inside the stand was cool and moist and mushroomy. I half-expected a tribe of cannibals to rush out and remove my head with a large machete, but except for the birds talking to one another, it was completely still. There was a clearing in the middle and I sat on the mossy ground and looked around. I tilted my head way back to see the tops of the trees stirring in the breeze, contrasting with the impossi-bly blue sky. It seemed as though the trees were still and I was the one moving. It made me dizzy. Finally I just laid back and took in the whole thing lying on the ground with my arms and legs spread-eagled. It really was so beautiful. I snapped a bunch of pictures lying on the ground like that, looking up. It felt to me that a lot of people before me had called this their secret spot. I pictured stolen kisses and the reading of love letters and members-only forts and kids dressed as pirates, tasting beer and cigarettes for the first time. I knew that this now belonged to me. This would be my place to hide.

The last thing Javier fixed before he moved on to his next job was the porch swing, which I'd found in the barn in rough shape. He sanded it and painted it and reattached it in the same place it was in that old photo. I took a new photo of the house. It was hardly transformed but it looked a lot better. Maybe I would hide the photo in a box one day too. My dad and I put big terra-cotta pots on both sides of each porch step, six in all, and planted red geraniums in them. I pulled the rocker from the living room out to the porch too. So now we had a choice: swinging or rocking. They both seemed like good places to sit and watch absolutely nothing happen.

7

$\mathcal{E}$ven though Storm says that it's inevitable that I'll run into Forest again and again, I like to believe there's a certain serendipity to it. Case in point: On my way into town the other day, I saw Skeeter Dumb-ass (real name Dumas, but trust me, he's earned his nickname) at the gas station, filling up his monster pickup with a lit cigarette dangling from his mouth less than a foot from the tank he was filling with highly combustible gasoline. I hadn't seen him in months and I probably won't see him for months now either (in the unlikely event that he should live that long). Anyway, my point is, even in a place this small, people travel in certain circles.

So far I've seen Forest at the hospital, the swimming hole, the farmers' market, and Millie's, and now I'm standing one aisle away from him at the grocery store, contemplating my next move as he thumbs through this month's *Rolling Stone* in the magazine section. In these situations, where you see a person of interest before they see you, it's advisable to take a moment to compose yourself before you saunter over and make it look like a crazy coincidence. I lurk next to the peanut butter and Cheez Whiz; unfortunately, I don't have much to work with here. I try to fluff my hair but it appears to be unfluffable and I can't recall when I washed it last. Damn! Note to self: Stop leaving the house looking like an Amish woman. I apply ChapStick, the only quasi–beauty product on me, and rub my lips together. I walk over to his aisle and pretend to be focusing on the magazines while I let *him* notice *me*. Storm would be proud.

"Hey, hi!" he says, smiling.

"Oh, hi!" I chirp. *Wait, was that too much? Not enough?*

"Whatcha doin'?" he asks.

I decide that he seems smart enough to know that I'm not shopping for a piano so he probably doesn't need an answer to that question. I glance down at my basket, which holds a package of linguine, black tea, and a bag of organic brown sugar. I thank God that I haven't hit the feminine products aisle yet. I decide not to tell him the primary reason I'm here and that is to buy a proper vase, not a canning jar like we usually use, to put flowers in the bunkhouse. Tomás arrives tomorrow afternoon to start work and I wanted to do something special. When I left the farm, Miguel was scrubbing the outdoor shower and Steve was working on the outhouse. I think we all want things to be nice for Tomás, although it's hard to imagine that it would make any difference to him, considering what he's been through. So far I haven't found a vase and I've pretty much given up hope. I'm not even convinced that flowers are the way to go. They might seem a little funereal at this point.

A shopping cart is parked next to Forest, piled high with microwave popcorn and bags of Doritos and soda. Maybe he is a little fuzzy on the whole concept of grocery shopping after all.

"So. Are you still enjoying country life?"

"Sure. I guess."

I look at the magazine he's reading. "Hey, did you read that piece on the Monsters of Folk?"

"Yeah. I'm just reading it now. Do you like them?"

"I do. I love Bright Eyes." I click on my MP3 player and hold one of the earbuds up to his right ear. It plays "The First Day of My Life." He grins.

"I love that song." He looks at me and I feel slightly elevated. I mean, what are the chances that I would just then be listening to a song by a band that contains two members of a band that he was reading about? It smacks of serendipity.

"Yeah, me too." I smile at him.

Forest looks at his cart and returns the magazine to

the rack. "I'm pretty much finished here. Do you wanna go somewhere or maybe go for a drive?"

"You have a car?"

"I wouldn't call it a car. But it'll do the job."

"I'm on my bike."

"We can throw it in the back. The trunk is very spacious; I'm contemplating moving in."

"Okay." I try not to think about how many of my dad's rules I'm violating. Not the least of which is I'm not supposed to get in a car with anyone under twenty-one. The prospect of knowing Forest better makes me feel reckless. If he asked me the right way, I'd probably run away with him right now.

Things get a little awkward at the checkout. Rita, the cashier, rings me up and I know that she knows just about everything about everyone in a one-hundred-mile radius. Small talk is unavoidable.

"So, I hear you've got Tomás coming to work at your place."

"Yup." I glance at Forest. He's perusing the gum.

"That's nice. I met him once. Sylvia was always in here picking up groceries with that sweet baby, Rosa. Nice family. Really awful what happened."

I nod. Forest's eyes shift over to me but he looks away quickly, pretending not to hear.

I get my change and say good-bye to Rita. If she knows

who Forest is, she's not letting on and he's certainly not offering. Outside, I stand next to my bike, putting my groceries in my backpack. I look up to see Brody Burk driving by slowly in his massive black truck. He watches me with an expression on his face that is obviously meant to unsettle me. His idiot twin sons are in the cab with him. His pit bull rides in the back, chained to the truck bed. He watches me in his side mirror and when I'm out of his sight he punches the gas, making the pit bull lose its footing. It yelps as the choke chain around its neck tightens. The hair on the back of my neck stands up.

Forest appears a minute later. He points to a rusted-out Ford, parked at the curb.

"Well?" He grins.

"This is your car?"

"Nah, it's my stepdad's. It's the only car he'll let me drive. I've only had my license for two months."

I cringe. *Two months?*

We wrestle my bike into the trunk. I pull open the whiny passenger door and get in next to him on the cracked vinyl seat. It smells like dust and motor oil. He throws his bag of groceries in the backseat and puts the key in the ignition, turns it, and pumps the gas. The engine finally roars to life. He pats the dash.

"She purrs like a kitten," he says over the roar of the engine.

"Do you think we'll make it?" I ask nervously.

"Sure, this baby has years left on her."

Darth Vader dangles from the rearview mirror, reassuring me. Forest backs out of the parking space and heads toward our farm.

"So, where to, country girl?"

"Please don't call me that." I glare at him. "I've lived in the city most of my life and it wasn't my idea to move here."

"Okay. Sorry. Where to?"

"Well, I had something planned for this afternoon but you can come along if you like."

"Okay. Tell me where to go."

Could it really be this easy? You spend hours daydreaming about someone and then suddenly you're driving down the road with him, going somewhere together, like you've known each other for years. I tell him to turn right at the next corner and he cranks the giant steering wheel like he's turning a river barge. We drive down a narrow road for about five miles and I point to the side of the road and tell him to pull over next to a little farm stand. We get out of the car and walk down an unmarked lane with lush stalks of twelve-foot bamboo growing on either side. Forest never once asks me where we're going. He walks silently next to me. I like that about him. We eventually come to a clearing and to the right of us two Buddhist monks in orange robes are bent over, tending a terraced vegetable garden built into the hillside. Their persimmon-colored robes contrast beautifully with the rich green of the garden and I stop and take a couple of shots with my camera, which is loaded with color film today. The monks see us and wave. I wave back. From this far away, I can't tell who they are because they all have the same shaved heads and even the old monks carry themselves like young men.

"They don't mind?" asks Forest.

"No. That's the thing about them. They don't mind anything as long as you respect them."

"Cool."

We continue on, veering off on a narrow gravel path that leads through a perfectly tended oriental flower garden. We cross over a wooden bridge with a koi pond underneath it. The big orange-and-black-speckled fish surface with their mouths open like baby sparrows. The monastery is quiet except for the sound of metal wind chimes that make a resonant musical sound, each tube a different note, not unlike the sound of chanting. A monk is sitting cross-legged on a wooden bench up ahead. He's reading a book. His sandals sit on the ground in front of him. He looks up and smiles.

"Hello."

We both say hello and carry on past a gazebo. The three-legged dog is napping on the cool floor inside it. He raises his head for a second, checking us out, and then goes back to his nap. Past the gazebo, the trail leads to a sparse dining room with a big kitchen, and then on to separate little residences for the monks and then the grand finale, a beautiful ornate temple where the monks pray and meditate. We pass by the back door of the kitchen, which is propped open with a stone. There are a couple of young monks baking bread. The aroma is intoxicating. Two of them stand across from each other, punching dough down on a big metal-topped island. When they see us, they bow their heads slightly in greeting and one of them beckons me over. He grabs a heavy serrated knife and cuts a couple of slices off a loaf that sits cooling on a rolling rack next to the island. He hands them to me, smiling. I nod my head in thanks and take the soft, moist slices. I hand one to Forest. He takes a bite.

"Well, that is about the best thing I've ever tasted."

I smile. "Isn't it? You can buy it at the grocery store in town, you know."

"Wow. This bread could change a person's life."

We walk along the path until we come to a bench that overlooks the property with the temple off to the right. Somehow, even on the hottest days, it feels cool here.

"You wanna sit?" I ask.

"Sure. Is it okay?"

"Yup. Like I said. They don't mind. I've been coming

here for a year and a half."

"This is the most peaceful place on earth," Forest says, sitting down and taking in the dramatic view. "What do I have to do to live here?"

"Give up all your worldly possessions and meditate eight hours a day." I sit down next to him and finish my bread, savoring the crunchy crust.

"Sounds reasonable. Do I get to eat this bread every day?"

"Yes, but the monks are vegan. And no Doritos, no soda, no microwave popcorn."

Forest looks sheepish. "Hey, thanks for bringing me here. This is incredible. Really, I'm loving it."

"You're welcome." I smile, happy that he knows that this place is special. Part of me thinks that maybe I brought him here as a test. If you want to know if you like someone, bring them to a sacred place and see how they behave. I snap a photo of him in profile just as he looks away.

"Am I going to have to start combing my hair?" he says, smirking.

"No. I'd hate that."

A kitten runs across my feet and puts on a show, chasing a fly for a few seconds. When she comes within reaching distance I grab her and put her on my lap. She attacks my fingers with her little paws and mews contentedly.

"All the smart animals end up here," I say, scratching the kitten's chin. "The monks take great care of them. No one goes hungry."

"How do the monks survive? Who pays for all this?"

"Well, this is a monastery but it's technically a working farm, just like ours. The monks sell a lot of what they grow, plus the bread, and they're famous for their jams too. You can also come here and take seminars. The monks teach people how to meditate and chant and find peace and recover from trauma and things like that. The land was a gift from a rich Californian who became a Buddhist and wanted to unload his material possessions. He lives here a lot of the time too."

"How do you know all this?"

I shrug. "I don't know. I just picked it up in bits and pieces. The monks aren't chatty but they're happy to answer a question or two."

We sit there for a long time. This place does that to you. It makes you lose track of time. When we finally make a move to leave I have no idea how long we've been here. On the way out of the monastery, we pass a wooden donation box. Forest pulls a couple dollars out of his pocket and stuffs them in. I'm pretty sure I would marry him on the spot.

We climb back in the car and I direct Forest to my farm. I ask him to let me out a safe distance away and he doesn't question it. We have yet to talk about his mother and what happened. There was that awkward apology at the farmers' market but I think that we should talk about the accident before it becomes that big, ugly thing that we don't talk about. But not today. Today was about something else. I give him my phone number and my email address and he gives me his and now we're connected. We know how to find each other. Everything from here on will be different.

As we're pulling my bike and my backpack out of the trunk Forest tells me he'd like to do this again. When he says it, he looks away as though he's afraid I'll say no.

"This? You mean the monastery?"

"No, I mean this going somewhere together thing. Can we do it again?"

"Sure." I smile and my mind races ahead to secret meeting spots, code words, nicknames, maps, letters, all of the things you do when you want to see someone and you have to keep it a secret. I wonder what I've gotten myself into but I know it's already too late to turn back.

I snap a photo of the back of his car bombing down the road away from me. As I lower my camera and stand there with my bike leaning against my thigh, I can see him watching me in his mirror and I know that I'm half in love with him already.

8

*T*omás materializes on the porch from out of nowhere. There is no car pulling away, or a bus, or a van, or anything. Rufus didn't even hear him until he tapped on the screen door. I open it to find him standing there, his straw cowboy hat in his hand and a small duffel at his feet. He looks as though he just strolled over from next door. His white shirt is crisp and freshly ironed and his jeans have a sharp crease down the front. He looks so much younger than I had imagined; he's really just a kid. Despite his smile, it's easy to see that he's in a lot of pain. My dad comes to the door and greets him in slow, soft Spanish. Tomás shakes his hand and thanks him for the job. My dad tells him that he's sorry for his loss. He shrugs and tilts his head slightly in that way that Hispanics do, meaning the intolerable must be tolerated. Pain is pain but work is necessary for life and, as farm labor goes, this isn't too bad. My dad gives his employees a comfortable place to sleep, a hot shower, fair pay; he doesn't expose them to any pesticides; and he even feeds anyone who happens to be around at dinnertime. We've heard horror stories lately about the overcrowded *colonias*, trailer parks with people sleeping wall-to-wall and in shifts. Some workers sleep in their cars if they own one and some even sleep in the fields where they work because they can't afford to rent a place. Since most of the workers are undocumented, paying them even minimum wage isn't required and a lot of farmers take advantage of that. When I asked my dad what happened to Wanda's husband, he shrugged and said no one really knows. Sometimes the coyotes, paid guides who escort Mexicans safely across the border, are crooked and they take your money and abandon you. Wanda's husband had paid a coyote but he never showed up on the other side. Wanda has accepted that the worst has probably happened. He was probably left to die in the hot desert.

My dad walks with Tomás in the direction of the bunkhouse, Tomás taking two steps for every one of my dad's long-legged strides. I'm glad that in the end I decided to put some lavender in there, even if it is in a canning jar. Tomás and my dad walk past the gossiping chickens pecking at the dirt and my dad points at them and then back at me, standing on the porch, watching. He might be telling him that the chickens are my job but he might also be saying, "Those are the chickens. They don't like my daughter much." Steve and Miguel form a friendly welcoming committee, walking over to shake hands, and even Rufus seems to have taken a shine to Tomás, trotting slightly ahead of him and looking back to make sure he's still there.

As I stand on the porch watching the four men and a dog make their way to the bunkhouse, I think about how perhaps some powerful otherworldly force may have brought us all together in this place. My dad and I lost someone, Rufus lost his family, and now, because Tomás has lost someone too, he ended up here with us. It's a crazy theory but maybe we were meant to find one another and help each other out or maybe I'm just overthinking this whole thing. Maybe Tomás is just grateful for a job and that's that.

I open the screen door and let it ease shut behind me. I take the stairs quickly up to my room and turn on my computer. My heart leaps at the sight of a new email from Forest. I open it.

To: Photogirl@earthlink.net
From: Hamonrye@yahoo.com
Subject: Get me out of here!

Roar,
It's my turn to take you somewhere now. Let's go to Berkeley and hunt for music. I found myself singing along with Air Supply at the mini-mart today. Rescue

me. We'll drink coffee and buy stinky incense on Telegraph Avenue. When can you go? The sooner the better.

Forest

I'm so pleased that he didn't use abbreviations like "U" and "R" for "you" and "are" or, God forbid, sideways smiley faces. Would I have eliminated him as a possible boyfriend if he'd written a bad email? Probably not, but I love that he didn't disappoint. I write him back immediately. We make a date for tomorrow and I'm definitely washing my hair tonight.

Early this morning I was up working in the darkroom, developing a roll of black-and-white film. The photo of Forest at the farmers' market was on the roll and I printed off an eight-by-ten. It's a classic candid. I've caught him in midstride, looking over his shoulder in my direction but not at the camera. His eyes are slightly narrowed. It could easily be a moody album cover. I'd forgotten about the one he took of me at Millie's. It's possibly the best photo anyone's ever taken of me even though I'm looking embarrassingly flustered. The color roll I shot at the monastery will have to wait. It has to be processed at the Looking Glass in Berkeley. I'll drop it off there tomorrow.

Storm is my alibi and she's been briefed. We're allegedly

going to a movie and her dad is dropping us off. My dad never asks for details so I should be okay. I don't address the weird feeling this deception is giving me. I've never really lied to my dad before. Storm is a willing accessory to the crime. She's absolutely giddy about the idea that I'm doing something subversive, and she's interrogated me endlessly about Forest.

"Does he have any tattoos?" she asked breathlessly.

"I don't know. None that I could see."

"Piercings?"

"I'm not sure. We had all our clothes on."

"Do you think he's circumcised?"

"How could I possibly know that?"

"Is he a good kisser?"

"We didn't kiss."

"Did he even touch you?" She became impatient.

"No." But the real answer is yes. It's just too abstract for Storm to understand. No, he didn't grab me around the waist or kiss me or jam his tongue in my mouth but his leg was next to mine when I sat with him on the bench at the monastery and it felt electric, and then, later, his hand brushed against mine when we took my bike out of the trunk and somehow it felt very intimate.

"Does he at least smell nice?"

I assumed she meant cologne of some sort. You can

always smell Storm's boyfriends before you see them. But I did notice that Forest smells a little like apples and a little like licorice. It's very subtle but I like it. I wonder what I smelled like to him. I hope it wasn't something farmy.

I also noticed the way his black hair falls across his sea-glass eyes in a chunk and the habit he has of removing it by raking it slowly back with his long fingers, and I noticed that his top lip comes together in two perfect little peaks and that his front teeth overlap ever so slightly. He also does this thing where he looks down shyly after he says something. That has to be my favorite thing about him so far.

Even though I think about Forest almost all the time, one thing I try not to think about is who his mother is. It seems impossible to me that the woman I saw that day on the road could possibly have given birth to someone like Forest, who doesn't seem at all like her. Maybe he's more like his dad in L.A., or maybe he's adopted.

At eleven a.m. the next morning, I'm sitting on a wooden fence near the swimming hole. My bike is locked up next to me already. Just a couple of minutes pass before I hear the roar of Forest's car. It sounds like something heavy on the spin cycle of a washing machine. He pulls up next to me and grins. I hop off the fence and slide in beside him like we're

Bonnie and Clyde on our way to a heist. He hits the gas and we're off.

An hour and a half later we're sitting at a table in the window of Caffe Med on Telegraph Avenue in Berkeley—a street famous for its tolerance of extreme weirdness—drinking hot lattes from enormous heavy mugs. We watch a steady stream of people walk by the window: Cal summer students; homeless people dressed in all the clothes they own, trying to outweird one another for spare change; and regular people, here to shop for books and music. From where we sit we can see a wide variety of customers coming and going from the tattoo parlor next door. A suburban woman pushing a baby carriage through the door illustrates the point that you no longer have to be an ex-con or a sailor or a gang member or even interesting to get a tattoo. The Med (short for Mediterranean) is famous for attracting an eclectic crowd. It's one of those places where you might run into a famous poet but you'd never use the bathroom. I'm happy to be sitting here with Forest. He seems comfortable in this place even though he says he's only been here a couple of times. I ask him about his life back in L.A. I'm eager to fill in the missing pieces.

"My dad's a psychiatrist. He married my mom when they were both pretty young. A few years ago, my dad got involved with one of his patients and everything changed."

"What happened?"

"Well, my dad believes in being honest about everything even if he knows it's going to hurt, so he told my mom and they separated. It practically killed my mom. She completely fell apart; she started self-medicating."

I'm all too familiar with the term.

"She started drinking and taking painkillers and talking about suicide. It was like everyone checked out of our family at once. I started doing a little self-medicating myself."

"With what?"

"I wasn't picky, whatever was laying around. Beer, Valium, pot, and then I started working my way through some of the finest Pinot Noirs of the Burgundy region that my dad kept in his wine cellar."

"Didn't your dad notice?"

"No, actually"—he looks down into his coffee cup—"not until the letters from school started arriving. School had become optional at that point."

"So, what happened?"

"I went to kiddie rehab."

"What was that like?"

"Stupid. A bunch of whiny, spoiled L.A. brats talking about their so-called problems. I was out in three weeks." Forest looks up and grins. "With a new outlook."

"What about your mom?"

"My mom eventually pulled herself out of it, got some help. She joined AA, got into the whole twelve-step thing, but I don't think she ever recovered completely."

"What about the patient your dad was seeing?"

"My dad divorced my mom and married her."

"So now you live with her when you're at home in L.A.?"

"Yeah. It's weird. I keep pretty much to myself when I'm there. My dad and I get along okay but his new wife is a lot younger than he is and she's not that keen on the idea of a teenage son hanging around. I was never part of her plan. She and my dad have a daughter, a wretched little girl named Felicity. She rules the household under a strict fascist regime."

"What about your stepdad? Do you get along with him?"

"Yeah, Jerry's a real prince. He and I stay out of each other's way. He was the first guy who paid any attention to my mom after my dad left her and they were married within a year. Jerry's a Realtor, in the worst possible sense of the word. That's how they ended up out here. He didn't do that great in L.A. Too much competition and he's got that creepy vibe. Out here he does okay."

I take a sip of my coffee. A man dressed in a jumpsuit made entirely of duct tape pounds on the window. He looks like a low-rent astronaut. He slowly licks the window with his brownish tongue and when we don't react he moves on, leaving a big smear on the glass.

"So," I ask carefully, not sure I want an answer, "how are things since . . . ?" I pause.

"Since the accident? Not so good." He looks away.

"I'm sorry. We don't have to talk about this."

"No, it's okay. I think we should."

I wait for him to continue. He takes a deep breath.

"Look, I'm sure that you've noticed that my mom's desperately trying to look like a cast member from *Baywatch*."

"Yeah, sort of."

"Well, she wasn't always like that. It's like she's trying to compete with my dad's new wife even though they're twenty years apart, and then, to add insult to injury, Jerry had a fling with the receptionist at his real estate office and my mom found out about it. The accident happened the next morning. There's no excuse for what she did. She just lost it, I guess, but she's a wreck now. Most days she turns the phone off and sleeps all day."

"But I saw her at the farmers' market."

"That was back when she thought she should get out there and face it. I don't think she feels that way anymore. I think most of the time she just lies there and thinks about how, if only she hadn't passed your dad's truck that day, if only she hadn't been in such a hurry, everything would be different."

It's hard for me to feel any sympathy for Forest's mom. I don't think that there could be anything that he could tell me that would help me understand why she did what she did, but I feel like she may not really be the person I saw that day. The woman I saw was so angry. After the accident, I'd imagined her going to her Pilates class, lunch with the girls, shopping, and just carrying on with her life like nothing happened. Now I know it wasn't like that.

I watch a young man with long dreadlocks roll by the window in a wheelchair. The back of his chair is plastered with Bob Marley stickers.

"So, what about you?" Forest asks.

"What do you mean?"

"C'mon, I know it's not *Little House on the Prairie* over there on the farm. Tell me everything."

"You sure? It'll take a minute."

"I've got a thousand." He leans back in his chair and looks at me expectantly.

I'm really glad he went first. Hearing Forest's story makes it so much easier to tell mine. I tell him about my former life in the city, my mom, and all the crap that's happened since she disappeared. I start with broad strokes but then I find myself filling in the small details. He listens to me, nodding with empathy at the right moments, but he never interrupts. When I'm finished he looks at me for a long time.

"Wow. I think you won that round."

"Nah, I think we're tied."

An elderly man with long, matted gray hair and wearing a threadbare overcoat sits down at the table next to us. The overcoat seems expensive. It's seventy degrees outside. He studies the two of us carefully for a minute as he stirs his coffee.

"Are you guys brother and sister?" he asks, interrupting our moment, and displaying his lack of dental care.

We both say no and it seems to hit us both at the same time that we may actually look alike: same hair color, complexion, pretty close on the eyes, although Forest's are greener and slightly tilted down at the edges. Forest's nose is long and straight and narrow. Mine has a bump right in the middle, like my mom's.

"Ya look just like each other," says the man. "Like Hansel and Gretel."

My version of Hansel and Gretel featured ultrablond Scandinavian kids, but still, it's funny and Forest grins at me.

"Maybe we were separated at the orphanage, huh?"

God, I hope not, based on what I've imagined doing with him.

The man busies himself with his sugar packets and Forest and I go back to our conversation.

"Do you ever hear from your mom?"

"Nope. Not so far."

"Do you want to?"

"I'd really like to talk to her. I mean, I don't hate her or anything. I think about her every day."

"You must really miss her."

"I miss the mom she was before she changed."

"And your dad too. He must miss her a lot."

"I don't know. It's become our elephant in the room. We don't really talk about it but he seems to have lost all interest in women since my mom. I think his heart is broken. The farm is sort of like an island he exiled himself to."

I tell Forest about Tomás coming to work for us and he visibly winces. I know he must have heard rumblings about my dad trying to rally a civil suit against his mom but I don't think we should talk about that. At least not right now. Why ruin a perfectly good afternoon? Besides, I can hardly believe how much I've told him already.

We walk down the avenue, stopping to browse the street vendors who sell jewelry, candles, tie-dye T-shirts, bumper stickers, incense, and pottery. I take some photos of the street people but they all want to be paid and I run out of dollar bills quickly. Forest buys me a brightly colored woven Guatemalan bracelet and ties it on my wrist. His gentle touch sends an electric current all the way down to my toes. Our last stop on the avenue is the record store, where we stock up on CDs. I get the Shins, the Decemberists, the National, and Feist. Forest buys Elvis Costello, Belle and Sebastian, Elmore James, Jimmy Rogers, Cassandra Wilson, and a Frank Sinatra album, which he tries to hide from me, but the cashier makes a big deal about it, causing Forest to blush deeply. I tease him endlessly.

"Hey, what can I say?" He smirks. "Frank moves me in mysterious ways."

We eat a late lunch at a Middle Eastern restaurant on College Avenue and head back home after I drop my color film off at the Looking Glass. In the car, I pull the Frank Sinatra out of the bag and grin at Forest mischievously as I remove the cellophane.

"Put that down, Gretel, you're not old enough."

I slide the CD into the player.

"I mean it now, you're playing with fire, young lady."

We drive along in the slow lane as Frank sings "Fly Me to the Moon."

9

$\mathcal{M}$y dad looks over his tiny gold reading glasses at me. He's sitting at the wooden kitchen table surrounded by books and pamphlets and photos. His pen is poised over a blank page in a lined notebook. My dad is not a computer person.

"What's up, honey bear?" he asks me as I slide into the chair across from him, wiping my forehead with the sleeve of my shirt.

"Those hateful chickens are fed and watered. The farm stand is stocked and the compost heap is turned and can you please tell Steve that his worn-out socks will not break down in the compost heap? I've told him a thousand times and he seems not to hear me."

My dad snorts and tries not to grin. I glare at him.

"Why is that funny to you? I swear it's like some sort

of male conspiracy out there." I get up from the table and yank open the fridge, pulling out a pitcher of chilled water and pouring myself a glass.

"Want some?" I hold up the glass.

"Sure."

I pull another glass out of the cupboard and put the water in front of him. I sit down across from him again.

"What are you doing?"

"Writing a speech. I'm speaking at a sustainable farming conference in Vermont this weekend."

"This weekend? When will you be back?"

"Monday night."

"Who's going to run this place?"

"Steve and you."

"Thanks for telling me." I sulk.

"Honey, it's not the Pentagon. You'll be fine. Jane's coming out for the weekend to stay here too, so you'll even have a woman to conspire with."

"Yeah, right. Her and Steve will be doing it all weekend while I do all the work."

"You know that's not true. Jane will take it very seriously."

Suddenly a lightbulb goes on in my head. If my dad's away I can have Forest over. I can talk to Steve and he'll keep it to himself. Jane will be cool and Miguel and Tomás definitely won't say anything. Plus, I'd like Forest to meet all these people. I don't think I should tell Tomás who Forest is just yet. Another bit of guilt washes over me.

I put my empty glass in the sink and glance out the window at the gardens outside. Tomás has proven himself to be a very good worker. Right now he's bent over a shovel, digging up beets and baby potatoes for the market and the restaurant deliveries. He works steadily and with purpose, jumping on the edge of the shovel with both feet and bending over to knock the dirt off the beets and then tossing them into the wheelbarrow.

"So, what's your speech about?" I ask, my mood lightening by the second.

My dad writes for a couple seconds and then lifts his head. "Educating restaurants and grocers on the benefits of buying directly from local and sustainable farms."

"You might want to throw in a couple of jokes to warm up the crowd."

"They don't need jokes. They're all farmers and they paid four hundred bucks to be there."

"Trust me, Dad. Everyone needs jokes."

I open the screen door and walk out onto the porch to sit in the rocker for a minute. Rufus is napping next to the porch swing, his body stretched out in the shape of a "U."

I pull my knees up to my chin and play with the

Guatemalan bracelet that Forest tied on my wrist yesterday. I gaze out at the farm and lose myself in yet another replay of the moment I had with Forest when we said good-bye at the swimming hole (which, by the way, we now call the tar pits). I was nervous and flustered, knowing that if a kiss was coming, that would definitely be the moment. I know enough about moments to know that they're delicate and fleeting and if you're not careful you can blow them to bits. We both got out of the car and I walked over to my bike and bent over to unlock it. As I stood up, Forest took me by the hand and pulled me closer till our faces were about four inches from each other. He let go of my hand and let his hands rest on the small of my back. He tilted his head and pressed his lips on mine and just sort of left them there for a second, waiting for me to catch up. I pressed back with my lips and let my hands go wherever they wanted. They settled into the slight curve just above his hip bones. I could feel the outline of his ribs through his shirt. The kiss only lasted a few seconds, but after he pulled away he kept his face close to mine and ran his fingers down my jawline. He didn't say anything and neither did I, until he got back in his car and I was on my bike. He told me he'd see me soon and he waved and drove away in one direction while I pedaled off in another, hardly able to move my trembling legs at all.

Even though that technically wasn't my first kiss, I scarcely remember anything about the few times I've been kissed before. Those kisses were all fumbling, awkward hands and lips that didn't know what to do with themselves. My kiss with Forest made every other kiss completely forgettable.

Out by the barn, Steve is adding oil to the tractor. He doesn't notice me until I'm right next to him.

"Hi, Steve." I stand next to the tractor, faking interest.

"Hey. I didn't see you there. What's up?"

"Um, I hear Jane's coming for the weekend."

"Yup. We're going to camp out."

"Great. Listen," I say, glancing up at the house. "I have this, um, new friend that I want to invite over but I don't think my dad would approve."

Steve screws the oil cap back on. "Who? That guy whose mom killed Sylvia?"

"Yeah, could you maybe not mention that around him?"

"What about Tomás?"

"Tomás doesn't have to know who he is. It would only hurt him."

Steve looks disapproving.

"I know, I know. It's complicated, okay?"

"Okay. I won't say anything." His voice takes on a protective big-brother tone. "Is this guy okay?"

"Yeah." I look down at my boots and blush.

"Okay. I think I get the picture."

"Thanks, Steve. I'm thinking about letting you listen to my new CDs."

"Terrific," he grumbles.

On my way back up to the house I pass by the open bunkhouse door. I never go in there, but a flash of color gets my attention and I poke my head in. On the little table where I left the lavender, there's a white candle burning in a glass jar. Next to that is a small photo of Sylvia in a silver frame, smiling and looking radiant in an embroidered white blouse. Silver hoops hang from her earlobes. Her shiny black hair is parted down the middle and pulled back tightly in a traditional style like Frida Kahlo wears her hair in some of her self-portraits. This must be an older photo. I remember that Sylvia's hair was cut short the day I saw her, the day her life was cut short. I can't even imagine how Tomás gets through the day if this photo of Sylvia looking very much alive is the first thing he sees when he wakes up. A rosary made of soft pink stones lies coiled next to the photo, arranged carefully so that the crucifix is faceup and touching the frame.

Taped to the wall at the end of the bunkhouse there's a poster of Cesar Chavez. I recognize him immediately because I studied him in middle school. He was a Mexican

American who founded the UFW, the United Farm Workers union, and fought tirelessly for farmworkers' rights. You can't live anywhere near the Mission in San Francisco without knowing who he was because they even named a street after him. He's a hero to all farmworkers, but a lot of people, including my dad, say that all the good that he did has been undone by conservative anti-immigration government. I suddenly feel like I'm intruding so I leave quickly.

Early (even by farm standards) on Friday morning, I say good-bye to my dad and assure him that everything will be taken care of while he's away. (He's thoughtfully composed an endless list of things that need attending to.) I tell him that I'll miss him a lot and resist the urge to shove him into the idling truck, where Steve waits in the driver's seat to take him to the airport. I even stand in the driveway and make a show of it, waving as Steve pulls onto the road and the old pickup disappears. I'm fifteen years old (nearly sixteen) and I'm almost completely unsupervised until Monday night! Rufus returns from escorting the truck to the road and we walk back to the house together, up the stairs and back to bed for another hour. When Steve gets back I have to do restaurant deliveries with him but Miguel and Tomás have them all packed and ready to go, so I can sleep until five minutes before Steve is due back. Thirty minutes into my hour, the phone rings. I jerk awake and dig for the phone under a pile of dirty clothes.

"Hello?" I try to sound alert in case it's my dad.

"It's me."

"Forest?"

"Yes, how many me's do you know?"

"What are you doing? It's early."

"I know. I couldn't sleep and then I remembered it was okay to call. It is okay that I called, isn't it?"

"Yes." I pull the phone under the quilt with me.

"What are you doing?"

"Um, I'm mending a fence on the back forty."

"You are?"

"No. We don't even have a back forty, and if we did, I doubt the phone cord would reach. Actually, I'm in bed."

"Oh God! I woke a farm girl? Somehow I wasn't picturing that."

"It's okay. I need to get up anyway. The ungrateful chickens need tending to."

"Wait. Stay where you are. I want to picture you there for a minute."

"Okay." I close my eyes and listen to him breathe. I hope he's not picturing me in a rumpled, oversize T-shirt and saggy boxers, which is what I'm wearing.

"What time can I come over?"

"How about six?"

"I'll see you then."

By five o'clock Steve and I are back from doing deliveries. I brought my stack of fresh CDs along and we had a pretty good time getting into all my new tunes. Music is a great motivator and we knocked out the deliveries in record time. By the time Forest is due to arrive I even have the house looking halfway decent, which is better than it's looked in months. Laundry is in the laundry room, books on the bookshelf, and papers in a neat pile. The compost bowl next to the sink has been emptied and all lingering farm odors have been banished with Telegraph Avenue incense.

The first thing Forest says when he gets out of his beast in the driveway is "Man, I love that farm smell."

Rufus is annoyed at having his nap interrupted but he gives Forest a proper greeting, sniffing his leg and wagging his tail. Forest pats his head carefully, like someone who's not around animals much.

"He probably smells L.A. It's really hard to get rid of that smell."

"He loves city people. He took to me instantly."

Jane is in the kitchen boiling baby potatoes fresh out of the ground and chopping dill to make a potato salad. She sees Forest arriving and walks out onto the porch for an introduction, wiping her hands on her jeans. She takes his hand in hers and I probably should have warned him that she has superhuman strength. Luckily she doesn't hug him. Her hugs can collapse your lungs. Steve has a tent all set up on a small stretch of grass just inside the apricot orchard and he's built a fire pit out of stones so they can pretend to camp. Jane even brought all the stuff to make s'mores. I introduce Forest to Steve and then I take him on a tour of the place. I'm not sure if he's even interested but I soon realize that he most definitely is, and he asks a million questions. I can't believe how little he knows about food, let alone growing food. I walk him over to the fig trees and pluck a ripe fig. I pull it apart with my fingers and give half to him. He puts it in his mouth and his eyes open wide.

"Wow. I've never tasted a fig before. It sort of tastes like sweet dirt."

"I know." I smile and eat the other half.

By the time we're finished, he's tasted most of the food we grow. His hands are black with dirt and his shoes are caked with mud. I've explained composting in full detail. It blows his mind that we take all of our weeds and vegetable trimmings and eggshells and coffee grounds and even newspapers and pile them up, and that pile magically turns into the rich soil that we grow the vegetables in. Once he's got the hang of composting, I explain companion planting (planting a variety of herbs, flowers, and vegetables that attract good pests and repel bad pests from our main crop), and rainwater reservoirs (catching the winter rain in underground tanks to use for summer irrigation). I'm starting to feel like a museum docent. I show him the greenhouse and the barn and the chicken coop and my darkroom, which interests him more than anything. The photo he took of me at the diner is clipped to the clothesline. He looks at it carefully and nods.

"Can I have that?"

"Of course." I unclip it from the clothesline and hand it to him.

He holds it carefully by the edges with his dirty hands. He looks at it so long that I ask him if he wants me to sign it.

It's weird how I sometimes resent being here on the farm and living the opposite of the life I'd imagined for myself, but when I show the farm to Forest, an unexpected sense of pride swells in me. I've helped create so much of what stands here today and it feels pretty cool right now.

I save the house for last. I'm not sure what he'll think of it. Surely it looks nothing like the houses he lives in. We walk into the kitchen, which is now filled with the aroma of fresh dill and onions and vinegar. Jane is chopping small red onions and singing along to an old Cat Stevens record she found in my dad's collection. A glass of red wine sits on the counter next to her. She found the case that Reynaldo left behind for us on his last visit.

Forest strolls from room to room as though the house were a farm museum, one of those places you can visit to see how the early pioneers lived without electricity or running water.

"Wow. This place is so cool," he says quietly, the floor-boards creaking under his feet.

All I can see is that this place could really use a coat of paint.

"Come on. I'll show you my room." I lead the way upstairs. I'm not about to waste all the tidying up I did. The sun is dipping and my room is filled with a pre-dusk light that seems to add a certain romance to it. He sits on the iron bed and runs his hand over my quilt.

"I've imagined you sleeping here." He leans over and smells the pillow. "It smells like you."

I sit next to him on the bed and we swing our legs in unison like children. Forest puts his arm around my shoulders. We both laugh. I hope he can't tell how nervous I am. I've never had a boy in my bedroom and I've never even come close to feeling this way. I feel like I could do anything right now if Forest did it with me. It's exhilarating and it's also a bit scary.

"Hey." He points to the photos on the desk. "Is that your mom?"

"Yeah."

He walks over and picks up a framed photo. The best one, I think.

"Wow. You could be sisters. She's so beautiful."

"I know."

We hear a rumbling outside and I walk over to the window and look out to see Miguel driving the tractor into the yard. Tomás is riding in the trailer filled with tools that follows behind. Forest stands next to me.

"Which one is Tomás?" he asks.

"He's the one in the trailer."

"He's so young. I never expected him to be so young."

"Neither did I."

We stand there for a moment, side by side, watching, as Tomás jumps out of the trailer and walks next to Miguel toward the bunkhouse.

Back downstairs, Jane is rinsing a bunch of green grapes under the faucet and putting them in a bowl.

"Hey, Forest, can you go outside and make sure Steve didn't burn the place down? Tell him that the food's almost ready. He should tell Tomás and Miguel too. And he needs to cut some weenie sticks."

"Weenie sticks?"

"Yeah, to roast the hot dogs on, or veggie dogs if you prefer." She holds up a package.

"Sure, okay." He looks at me.

"I'm gonna help Jane carry the food out. I'll see you out there."

We wait for the screen door to wheeze shut before we say anything.

"So?" says Jane, eyebrows arched.

"So what?" I grin at her.

"So, he's pretty cute," she says, wiping her hands on a dish towel.

"He is, isn't he?"

"And nice. He's a nice boy."

"Did Steve tell you who his mother is?"

"He did. But luckily I don't believe in guilt by association. I go primarily on my spidey senses and I like him. Now, can you pull that corn out of the pot and wrap it up in foil?"

I find the tongs and pull the foil out of the drawer. "So, I guess you heard about what's going on around here."

Jane leans against the counter and grabs her wineglass. "More or less. Do you think your dad's going to go ahead with a lawsuit?"

I shrug. "Probably. He's not likely to leave this alone."

Jane muses, "No."

"You think my dad's nuts?"

She takes a sip. "No. He's not nuts. I'm not sure how

all of this will play out, though. Are you worried about it?"

"Yeah, I guess I am . . . a little."

"Well, you know, the thing about people like your dad is that you can't stop them from doing what they think is right, and it's probably a damn good thing that they don't think twenty steps ahead like some of the rest of us or they'd never try to change the world."

"Yeah, I know. It's just that it's my world too, you know? He dragged me out here, against my will, and now that I'm finally settling in, he's going to turn the entire town against us."

"Well, maybe not the entire town." She smiles. "C'mon, sweetie, let's not be glum, let's have fun tonight."

Jane and I work together to get all the food for our cookout into containers. I gather up forks and knives and plates and napkins and cups and condiments. Cat Stevens sings "Here Comes My Baby" as we head out the door, our arms piled high.

The light stays with us until the last hot dog is eaten. Rufus is only too happy to lick the plates. Darkness closes in around us and the stars appear. The fire turns everyone's face a warm golden brown. Jane explains how s'mores work to Miguel and Tomás. They've never seen them before but they seem to like them a lot. Jane's Spanish is pretty good and Steve can fill in whatever she misses. Forest is a bit of a rookie to this whole campfire concept too. Apparently he never went to camp. His first two hot dogs ended up as charred husks that even Rufus wouldn't eat and then I showed him how to brown them slowly, rotating the stick like a rotisserie over the very top of the flame.

Steve disappears from our circle for a couple of minutes and returns with a guitar. He plays around for a while, banging out bits of songs, and then he sings "Me and Bobby McGee," playing along while Jane sings harmony on the verses. He and Jane are experts at this; they camp all the time. They have a whole repertoire of campfire songs that they know. Reynaldo's wine is flowing and everyone has a glow to their cheeks. I pick up my camera and take some close-ups of Forest and then of Jane and Steve. When I take a photo, I try to catch the person in an unguarded moment. This isn't always easy. You have to be very patient but the result is worth it. Sometimes I pretend to take the photo and then I take the real one later when the person has forgotten about the camera. I ask Steve to ask Tomás if it's okay if I take a photo and Tomás nods shyly. I take a few of him and then a couple of him and Miguel. They have matching straw cowboy hats and Tomás is wearing a T-shirt advertising a toxic fertilizer company. Steve hands his guitar to Miguel, who fingerpicks a beautiful Mexican folk song. They call them *corridos* in Mexico. Miguel sings in that mournful way that Mexican folksingers have. Steve and Jane get up and slow dance in the grass next to us. Tomás sings along softly and I notice that Forest can't keep his eyes off of him. He seems to be watching his every move, studying him, memorizing what he looks like. After Miguel sings a few more songs, he hands the guitar over to Tomás. While I'm cursing my parents once again for never giving me music lessons, Tomás starts in on a heartbreaking love song in a voice so heavy with sadness that we all gape at him. Jane and Steve sit back down on their log and lose themselves in Tomás's voice. I forget to breathe. I brush away the tears that start to roll down my cheeks and I glance over at Forest. He's crying too but he's not wiping his tears away. He doesn't care if I see him. I take his hand in mine and squeeze it and we watch Tomás tell his sad, sad story, not understanding a word he's singing but understanding everything.

10

$\mathcal{T}$he morning sun in my eyes wakes me. I forgot to close my curtains last night. I lie there listening to familiar voices floating in through my open window. The clock on my bedside table says seven fifteen. My bedroom already feels warm. We're in for a hot day. Rufus has vacated the rug next to my bed, where he was passed out the last time I saw him. I kick off the covers and make my way to the window, yawning and scratching. The first thing that strikes me as bizarre is Forest's car. It's parked on the driveway in virtually the same place that it was parked yesterday. I did say good-bye last night and he did leave, didn't he? The voices I heard belong to Forest and Steve and Tomás. They appear to be loading the pickup for the local market today. Forest is carrying a box of beets over to the truck, his pale, lean arms straining. He and Tomás are laughing about something, which is also strange since they don't even speak the same language. I watch Forest hand the box off to Tomás. I am absolutely lovesick for this boy. As I watch him, I relive the kissing, the *real* kissing we did late last night when I walked him to his car. When he finally left I was dizzy for him.

And then he looks up and he sees me and he smiles.

I pull on my grass-stained jeans and a clean T-shirt and brush my teeth in four seconds. My hair is hickory smoked and tangled and my lips are pink around the edges from Forest's kisses. I yank my hair back into a ponytail and run down the wooden steps and out the front door as though the house were on fire. The boys watch me, amused.

"Hey, sleepyhead, nice of you to join us," says Forest.

"That's pretty big talk for someone who says that he never gets up before ten."

"I just thought I'd come over and help out. It's such a beautiful day."

I look from Forest to Steve, who shrugs. He looks a little bleary-eyed, possibly from polishing off half a case of wine between the four of them last night.

"Whaddya mean 'help out'? You came here voluntarily?"

"Well, yes, but a coffee would be nice."

"Okay." I'm mystified. Why would Forest just show up here, wanting to work? Does he need something to do or is this some sort of male bonding thing that girls aren't supposed to understand? It also occurs to me that this could be some form of penance he's serving on behalf of his mother. To sweat alongside Tomás might somehow make him feel better about everything.

"Where's Jane?" I ask Steve.

He heaves a box of Early Girl tomatoes into the back of the truck. "She went back to bed when Farmer Forest here showed up. She's a little under the weather." He mimes drinking wine.

"I'll bet."

"She'll be up shortly. That tent turns into a solar oven as soon as the sun hits it. You could roast a chicken in there."

I automatically glance over at the chickens. As a rule I don't like them to hear stuff like that. They're busy mumbling and pecking, oblivious.

"Okay, well, I'll go make that coffee." I glance at Forest again, confused.

I pull open the screen door and go back into the house and fire up the espresso machine. The machine was already used this morning and the remains of breakfast sit next to the sink. How did I sleep through people eating breakfast in my kitchen? I grind the espresso beans and fill the little cup with fragrant grounds, click it into place on the machine, and yank the heavy handle all the way to the right.

Thirty seconds later, thick, foamy coffee sputters into the mug below the spout. I fill a metal pitcher with cold milk from the fridge and open up the steamer knob, frothing the milk to three times its original volume. As I'm doing this, I watch out the kitchen window. Forest is following behind Tomás, pushing a wheelbarrow toward the zucchini and eggplant patch. Tomás seems rather amused by all this.

As I'm spooning the hot, foamy milk onto the coffee, I notice Forest's book bag slumped on a chair. I glance out the window. Forest is busy in the patch. My curiosity gets the better of me. I walk over to the book bag and flip it open, peering inside without touching anything. There are five notebooks, identical to the one I saw him writing in that day at the tar pits. I carefully slide one out. It's thick with writing. I slide it back into place, too overcome with guilt to open it. I also think for just a second about that scene in *The Shining* where Jack Nicholson has spent every day typing his "novel" and every line on every page of a huge stack of paper reads: "*All work and no play makes Jack a dull boy.*" I look behind me. No crazy person with an ax.

Next to the notebook there's a paperback: *Ham on Rye* by Charles Bukowski, Forest's email address, I get it now. I open it to the first page and read the opening sentence: *The first thing I remember is being under something.* I close the book and put it back in its spot. There's also a thin, white, official-looking book in there. I slide it out and look at the cover. It's a class schedule for NYU, New York University. Clear across the country, a million miles away. You don't carry class schedules around with you for nothing. He must be thinking about applying there. He hasn't said anything to me about it, but then why should he? Maybe this thing we have is just a summer fling to him; maybe if it weren't me it would be some other girl. After all, he's only here for the summer and then he's back in L.A. so it's not like a big commitment or anything. But then why would he be in my garden picking zucchini right now?

I dump a couple of spoons of brown sugar into the coffee and stride outside with it. On the way over to Forest, Steve tells me that he and Jane are going to do the market today so I'm off the hook. It's been ages since I've had a Saturday off. I wonder if Forest wants to do something with me or if he's planning hard labor for the rest of the day, or the rest of his life.

I catch up with Forest and hand him the mug.

"Caffeine at last." He takes the mug and sips it eagerly. A foamed milk mustache appears on his upper lip. He licks it off but doesn't quite get it.

Tomás tips his hat a bit and wishes me a good morning. "*Buenos días*, Aurora."

"*Buenos días*, Tomás. How are you?"

"*Muy bien*, very good." He says the English words quietly just as I do with my Spanish words.

I turn my attention back to Forest. "So, I have the day off. Jane's taking my market shift. How long till farm life loses its appeal for you?" I notice that his pale skin is starting to turn slightly pinkish. I poke him in the arm with my index finger. It leaves a white dot. "You're burning, by the way."

"Let me just finish loading the truck and then I think I'll have a whole new appreciation for farmwork, okay?"

"Sure." I walk away as Tomás has a good laugh at Forest's expense. He doesn't need to speak English to know what's going on here.

After I put Band-Aids on Forest's blistered palms and loan him a long-sleeved T-shirt, we're ready to go back outdoors. Jane and Steve are long gone and Miguel and Tomás are off with the tractor somewhere.

"Where are you taking me? You know I've already put in a good day's work so let's not get carried away," says Forest, following me.

"It's nine a.m., you worked for exactly two hours."

"Really? It's only nine a.m.? I could use a nap."

I roll my eyes at him. Out behind the greenhouse, I look for a sort of trail where I've tamped the grass down. I finally find it and set out. Forest walks behind me. Rufus quickly loses interest. He trots back to the house to pretend he's a guard dog.

We walk along in silence. I don't ask him about why he came over this morning to work. If he wants to tell me, he will; otherwise, it's his business. I'm more concerned with prompting Forest to talk to me about NYU and his plans for the future but I'm afraid he'll think I want more than he's prepared to give. I'm also afraid that if I say anything, he'll know I went through his things, which I'm feeling a little ashamed about.

In a few minutes we arrive at the stand of trees, the impromptu forest. How could I not take Forest here? He's named after it.

"Wow. What is this place?" asks Forest, his mouth agape, looking up through the trees.

"I don't know. I think it used to be cleared ranchland and the rancher must have kept this little place intact so that his cattle had a place to stay cool and drink water. There must be a spring or something underneath us because I found some little pools of water."

"It's sort of like a natural cathedral, isn't it?"

I snap a photo of Forest looking up at the shards of light streaming down through the trees. It looks a bit like he's watching an alien spacecraft come in for a landing.

"How often do you come here?"

"Just sometimes. When I want to be alone."

"Do you ever come at night?"

"No. I bet it's supercreepy at night."

"No, I bet it's really cool at night."

"Maybe."

We hear a loud crack and follow the noise upward. It's a hawk, taking off from the limb of a pine tree. He's so close and well lit that you can see his giant talons lift off. Broken twigs flutter to the ground. His wingspan is enormous and he seems to fly so slowly, like a prehistoric bird in a film about dinosaurs. We can even hear the air rushing under his wings. I photograph him in full flight.

"Okay, that was pretty surreal."

"It was, wasn't it?"

We walk to the center of what I imagine to be a circle, where the moss is bright green and soft.

"Lay down next to me. It's really incredible."

We lie down next to each other, shoulders touching, and look up at the sky.

"You're right," says Forest.

He takes my hand in his. We stay like that for a while and then he rolls over and rests his head on his elbow, watching me.

"Roar, you're about the most amazing girl I've ever met."

"Get outta here." I laugh.

"I mean it. I don't know anyone else like you."

"When do you have to go back to L.A.?" I ask, completely destroying the moment, like an idiot.

"I don't know. I mean I do know but I don't want to think about it."

"I need to know how much time we have left."

"Fair enough. I'm supposed to go back on August thirtieth."

I do the math lightning quick. "That gives us six weeks."

"Yeah. I guess we'd better not waste a moment."

He leans over and kisses my neck. I close my eyes and let the light through the trees dance on my eyelids. Six weeks doesn't seem like nearly enough time to get to know absolutely everything about someone. Plus, August thirtieth is my birthday.

11

$\mathcal{M}$y dad arrives home late Monday night with a case of organic maple syrup and a head full of new ideas that he's only too happy to share with me the next morning as he savors his first good latte in days. (I think he missed that machine a lot more than he missed me.) While my dad dazzles me with his discovery of eight new varieties of heirloom potatoes, I flip through the mail and make a small stack of bills in front of him just to remind him that we're running a farm, not a potato museum. In among seed catalogues and a Slow Food quarterly, I discover a big manila envelope addressed to my dad. The return address says Ned Levine, Attorney-at-Law. Around here we call him Uncle Ned. He's a lawyer by day and a banjo player by night. He lives in the next county with a woman named Arden who shaves her head and keeps honeybees. Ned looks about as much like a lawyer as my dad, which is not at all.

"Hey, Dad. What's this?" I slide the envelope across the table.

My dad peers at the return address. "Oh, that must be the civil suit we're filing."

He says it like it's an L.L.Bean catalogue.

"The civil suit? You're going ahead with that?"

"Yes, of course. Did you think we'd just forget about it?"

"You mean Tomás and Wanda said it was okay?"

My dad tears the envelope open and pulls out a thick stack of papers. "Yes, they said it was okay. But the suit was filed in Tomás's name, and Rosa's, the baby. It's better that way because Rosa was born here so she's a citizen."

"Wait, so Tomás can file a civil suit even though he's not American?"

"Sure, anyone has access to our legal system. You don't have to be a citizen."

"So, what happens now?" I ask. All the moisture in my mouth seems to have disappeared.

"Well, Tomás lost his wife and the mother of his baby because Connie Gilwood was driving recklessly. They have a very good case. I'm pretty sure that the insurance company will want to settle out of court and the settlement will be enough for Tomás to go home and raise his daughter, and Wanda can quit her job at that factory farm where she's exposed to pesticides all day."

"Dad, are we doing a good thing here? I mean, it's about

more than the money, right? It's about getting rights for the farmworkers . . . isn't it?"

"Of course it is, Roar. The farmworkers aren't disposable. You can't just kill a human being and hope it all goes away just because that person isn't in the country legally. There has to be some kind of retribution."

"So, those papers are the same ones that are going to Connie Gilwood?"

"Yup, she's probably reading them right now." My dad tips his mug and drinks the last of his latte.

My stomach drops. I have to talk to Forest. He'll think I knew all about this and I have no idea why I didn't. It all happened right underneath my nose but maybe I was too busy sneaking around with Forest to pay attention.

It's not that I don't understand that this lawsuit is the right thing to do for Tomás and Wanda. I know that a settlement will make their lives better, but it won't bring Sylvia back. My dad is doing something that's rarely, if ever, been done. Mexican farmworkers just don't sue Americans. I know that this lawsuit will bring a lot of attention onto us, attention I don't want. My dad, on the other hand, lives for stuff like this. He's been fighting for the little guy for as long as I can remember, and he usually wins, but I don't know about this one. This one could be different. We live *here* now. These people are not like city people. They're not likely to take kindly to being told what's right by some hippie lawyer, fresh from the city, who now calls himself a farmer.

My dad gets up and puts his mug in the sink. "Oh, and another thing, you'll probably get called as a witness."

"What does that mean?" I ask, wide-eyed.

"It's no big deal. You just go to a sort of interview and tell them what happened that day in your own words."

"Why can't you do it? You were there too!"

"They'll probably consider me too biased to be a reliable witness. I've defended farmworkers in court. Don't worry about it. It'll be a breeze."

My dad walks out the door whistling and leaves me sitting there, stunned. It's bad enough that my boyfriend's mom is being accused of wrongful death by my dad, but now I'll be the one pointing the finger at her when the lawyer asks if the woman who killed Sylvia Rodriguez is in the courtroom. At least that's the way it happens on TV.

I go upstairs and check my email. There's nothing from Forest but there's another email from Storm, who I've been neglecting terribly. She's quick to point that out.

To: Photogirl@earthlink.net
From: Stormyweather@AOL.com
Subject: I hate you

Roar,
This is the third (and final) email I'm sending you. I

haven't heard from you in days. Where the hell have you been? BTW, I've met someone, a ranch hand from Stockton. He thinks I'm nineteen. He rides bulls in his spare time . . . BULLS! My parents HATE him, naturally. Call me if you haven't been abducted or something.

S.

P.S. Are you still extra-virgin?

I grab the phone and dial Forest's cell. There's no answer. I dial his home phone even though I don't want to. It rings seven times and then a man picks up. Jerry, I presume.

"Hi, may I speak to Forest?"

"Did you try his cell phone?" He sounds annoyed.

"Yes, there was no answer." I swallow, embarrassed at admitting that maybe Forest is avoiding me.

"Hang on." He covers the phone and yells.

I hear a click on the line. "I've got it," says Forest.

Jerry hangs up after sighing audibly.

"Hi," I say quietly.

"Hi," he says, same volume.

"Sorry to call you on this line but I really needed to talk to you."

"It's okay. We just got home."

"From where?"

"The hospital. My mom took a bunch of sleeping pills."

"Oh no! Is she all right?"

"She will be. The doctors say she's resting comfortably, which seemed rather obvious to me, considering she just swallowed a handful of sleeping pills."

"This is all my fault," I say, pulling myself into the fetal position on top of my quilt.

"What do you mean?"

"I didn't tell you about the lawsuit but I swear I didn't know. No one told me."

"What lawsuit?" he says, and I want to die.

"Um, look. We need to talk. Can you meet me at the tar pits?"

"When?"

"I can be there in fifteen minutes."

"Okay. I'll see you there."

Unfortunately, my bike is in the shed so I have to walk past my dad and Steve, who are busy revolutionizing the world of sustainable farming.

"Where are you off to?" my dad asks as I ride past them on my bike.

"Just a ride." I pedal like the Wicked Witch of the West, trying to avoid any more questions about where I'm going.

"If it's exercise you're after, you can bring the seedlings up from the greenhouse."

"I'll do it later," I yell over my shoulder.

Why can't Steve do that? Why is it that my dad always has some backbreaking task at the ready whenever he sees me without a tool in my hand? Has he forgotten our agreement?

As I bump along the road to the tar pits I try and sort out my thoughts for Forest so that I don't come off looking hysterical. I take deep breaths and arrange my features into calm like the monks at the monastery, who actually *are* calm instead of just trying to appear that way.

Forest is already there when I arrive and he's sitting cross-legged on the sand by the water, writing in his notebook. He turns around when he hears my bike on the gravel. He looks grim. I walk over and sit down next to him on the fake beach.

"I'm really sorry about your mom," I start.

"Yeah. Thanks." He puts his notebook in his book bag. "It's Jerry. He lied about breaking it off with the receptionist. She called my mom at home and told her everything. Apparently Jerry has been telling her that he's going to leave my mom and run away with her. I guess even *she* finally figured out that he was full of crap. She's twenty, by the way."

"So why would your mom try to kill herself over that guy?"

"I don't think she was really trying to kill herself. I

133

think she was just trying to get his attention. Anyway, she's so messed up right now, I really doubt she's thinking straight." He runs his fingers through his hair.

"Sorry. I'm so sorry." I look out over the water and swallow hard.

"So, what did you mean about a lawsuit?"

"Yeah, um. Tomás is suing your mom for wrongful death. She should get the papers today sometime." I hesitate. "Or, that is, when she's out of the hospital."

"Oh."

"I'm sorry. I didn't know, I just found out."

"Stop saying you're sorry."

"I can't."

"Look, my mom knew that this might happen. I'm sure she wasn't expecting all this to just disappear. I know it sounds crazy but now that someone is actually calling her on it, now that she's not getting away with murder, maybe it'll be okay."

"Really, you think so?"

"I don't know. People can go insane waiting for the other shoe to drop. You know what I mean? Guilt can make you do crazy things."

"I guess that's true. Do you think she'll leave Jerry?" I scoop up sand in the palm of my hand and let it flow through my fingers.

"I hope so. She'll have to work through it on her own. She used to be a really strong person, full of opinions and ideas. I like to think that that person is still in there somewhere."

"Did you tell your dad what happened?"

"Yeah. He's on his way out here. That should be interesting."

"Do you think he can help your mom?"

"No, but he can do his psychiatrist thing on her and get her thinking straight. You should meet him. I want you to."

"Okay. And, about the lawsuit, my dad says that your mom's insurance company will probably settle and there won't even be a trial. So it's not like she'll go to jail or anything like that."

"Really?"

"Uh-huh." I decide not to tell him that I'll probably be called as a witness. I'll wait on that little bombshell. He doesn't need to know that today.

We sit there, side by side, for a minute, looking out at the dark water. An orange dragonfly hovers above the glassy surface, buzzing from one side of the pool to the other, touching down here and there. Finally, Forest puts his arm around my shoulders and I lean into him, sliding my arm around his waist. We stay like that for a long time.

Later, at home, I make my famous black bean chili and set the table for me and my dad and Steve. Miguel and Tomás have gone off to a bar where farmworkers gather to listen to Latin music and drink a couple of cervezas and unwind. There's a real taqueria next door to it where they make Mexican food that tastes like the kind they get at home. The owners leave their Christmas lights on all year-round and the floor is covered in peanut shells.

My dad and Steve are vegetarians and Miguel and Tomás are not, and although they're really polite about it, I'm sure the crumbled vegetable protein I've got searing in the frying pan isn't very appealing to them. It's supposed to taste "just like ground beef" but no matter how many spices I dump on it, it never really comes close. Who do they think they're kidding? I slice some tomatoes I just picked that are still warm from the sun and toss them into the pan. The liquid in them sizzles when it hits the heat. I simmer the mixture for a while and then add it to the black beans and tomato sauce I've got cooking in a big pot. Steve comes in with an armload of baby greens and dumps them on the counter. He mixes up a quick olive-oil-and-lemon dressing in our big wooden salad bowl, whisking it with a fork, and tosses the greens in.

"Voila." He holds up the bowl for me to see and then sets it in the middle of the table. He pours himself a glass of water and sits down at the table while I fill big bowls with chili.

"Where's my dad?" I plop a bowl in front of Steve, prison-style.

"He's coming." Steve sniffs the chili. "Yum."

My dad comes in the house a couple of seconds later and scrubs his hands at the sink. He dries them on the kitchen towel while looking out the window over the sink.

"Anyone want wine?" he asks, looking at Steve, who raises his hand like a grade-school kid with the right answer.

My dad goes to the pantry and comes back with a bottle of Reynaldo's wine. Steve suddenly looks very interested in his chili.

"You guys got into the wine pretty good while I was gone," says my dad, pulling the corkscrew out of the drawer.

"Yeah. That was Roar. She went a little crazy."

I kick him hard under the table.

"Ow!" He rubs his shin.

My dad ignores us and pours himself and Steve a tumbler of wine.

I eat my chili quickly. I'm in no mood for my dad or Steve tonight. I've got a lot on my mind and it's nothing I can discuss at the dinner table. They don't really need me there anyway. My dad is still bubbling over with new ideas he wants to share with Steve. Plus, the deal around here is, if you cook you don't have to clean up. I put my bowl in the sink and feed Rufus out on the front porch, pouring a little black bean chili over his dog food like gravy. He stands there with his tail wagging. Rufus loves beans, but my bedroom will be filled with toxic gas tonight.

I go upstairs and close my bedroom door. I fall onto my bed and dial Storm's cell phone number. She picks up after several rings.

"Jesus! Where have you been?" she says without even saying hello.

"Sorry, I've got a lot going on. What are you doing?"

"I'm out shopping for a new best friend. Lucky for you, I haven't found anything I like yet."

"So, what's going on with you? Are you still dating the Marlboro Man?"

"Yeah. I think it's getting serious. He gave me a gold horseshoe necklace last night. It has a little diamond in it that you can only see under a microscope."

"Really?"

"Really. I think he got it at Wal-Mart."

"Do you like him?"

"Well, he's a lot of fun, and he's awfully cute. He says 'dang' all the time like it's a word. How cute is that?"

"Don't you think you should tell him your real age?"

"Are you kidding me?"

I sometimes forget that Storm plays with boys the way a cat plays with a ball of string. This relationship could be over tomorrow.

"Anyway," she says, "enough about me. Tell me what you've been up to and lie if you have to."

I sigh heavily and give her the whole story about my weekend with Forest, his mom, the civil suit, the witness thing, everything. Storm reacts in all the right spots but she's most interested in whether Forest and I have gotten to third base yet. I never know which base is what, though. I've never even seen a baseball game.

"If you're asking if I'm still a virgin, the answer is yes."

"Well, I'd be lying if I said I wasn't a little disappointed."

"I'll bear that in mind, Storm. You know how much I hate to disappoint you."

Storm and I make a plan to meet at the tar pits the next morning for a swim and I hang up the phone not feeling much better about anything. I lay there on my bed, watching the evening breeze ruffle my curtains through the window. The air smells like cool rosemary and sweetgrass and the weeds Steve pulled today. I hear Rufus climbing the stairs to my room and I get up to let him in. He sticks his face in mine and breathes dog-food breath all over me. Then, in a gesture of thanks for the meal I just served him, he licks me on the lips with his big pink tongue. Then he burps a mixture of black bean chili and dog food into my face. If that's not love, I don't know what is.

I suddenly remember that thing that Forest said about wanting me to meet his dad. That seems kind of serious. He wouldn't introduce me to his dad unless he was planning on knowing me for a while, would he?

"What on earth will I wear?" I ask Rufus, but he's busy with his post-dinner hygiene session, which I can't even watch.

From my bed I can see my entire pathetic wardrobe hanging in the closet. On the floor, there's a pair of white leather knee-high go-go boots with stacked heels that used to belong to my mom. Sometimes the boots make me miss my mom more than her photo does.

I wish she were here right now to help me decide what to wear. I wish she were here so I could say to her, "I met a boy."

12

My mom always kept a tube of Chanel lipstick on a little table near the front door of our house. Her shade was Shanghai Red. A little tin mirror with a silver peacock attached to the top of it hung directly above the table. The last thing she would do as she was going out the door was expertly apply her lipstick. She had the kind of coloring that comes alive with red lipstick. It made her eyes dance and her skin look like porcelain. She also had a vast collection of vintage sunglasses, which she shopped for relentlessly in secondhand shops and at garage sales. She had every shape and color you could imagine, including plaid and leopard print. She also had a couple of cat's-eye pairs with little rhinestones at the temples. One pair that I remember loving more than the rest had a large, squareish cream-colored frame and amber lenses. Whenever she wore those, she would tie a silk scarf around her black hair so that she looked like someone who lived on the Italian Riviera and drove around on a Vespa saying, "Ciao, *bella*!" Of course this was all before she changed into someone else.

Back then my mom and I always delighted in dressing up. Every time we stepped outside the house we saw it as another opportunity to be someone else. My mom never edited my outfits. If I showed up at the breakfast table in a bathing suit, knee-high vinyl boots, and a gorilla mask, she would smile and ask me what I'd like to eat.

My mom was a great playmate. Nothing was too messy or too hard or too silly for her. If we made anything to eat, no matter how simple, we always pretended that we were taping a cooking show and we'd look up and address our studio audience as we tutored them in the fine art of peanut-butter-and-jelly sandwiches. If we got on an elevator, we'd pretend to be spies, and a trip to the playground was an important archaeological dig. A nature walk was always an Andean or an Arctic expedition narrated by me or my mother, in a British accent.

For reasons I never understood, my mom refused to buy me any dolls. She told me that she didn't like the gender roles imposed on little girls by encouraging them to "play house" or take care of fake babies. I did own a few dolls, though. I bought them myself with my allowance at garage sales and secondhand stores, the same places my mom found her sunglasses. I treated them as though they were little mannequins. Instead of playing with them I would dress them up in outfits designed from scraps of fabric and costume jewelry and toilet paper. I would pose them around a little table piled high with food and plastic farm animals on little platters, as if they were posing for a Dutch master to paint.

Before I started school, my mom would take me out to art galleries all over the city and we would walk from one painting to the next, my mom looking at each painting carefully, from one angle and then another, the way an art critic might. She would say things like, "Well, technically it's quite accomplished but it lacks soul. It's not speaking to me." She said this with such authority that it always drew raised eyebrows from the gallery worker, who probably had a hard time believing that a real art critic would travel around with a five-year-old dressed in a tutu and rubber rain boots.

After my mom started painting, she couldn't go inside those galleries anymore. I don't think she could bear to compare her work to an artist's who had already made it to a gallery showing. I think it reminded her of how far she had to go. Her ego was very fragile. Besides, by then I was in school for several hours a day, so she had no one to go with. As I got older I started to understand that my mom and I were quite different. She wanted to be in front of the camera and I wanted to be behind it.

The white platform go-go boots were the only piece of my mom's clothing I took with me to the farm. She bought them in a consignment shop on Haight Street for twenty dollars. She claimed she was practically stealing them. I remember thinking, on the day that we left the city, that they were just too fabulous to leave behind. Now, when I look at them sitting there in my closet, cracking and gathering dust, next to my flip-flops and sneakers and work boots, they look absurd. It's hard to believe that the woman who gave birth to me once considered those boots a go-to item in her "casual" wardrobe. The longer I go without seeing her, the harder it is to imagine her in those boots.

Shortly after we moved to the farm, I completely lost interest in fashion. It seemed silly to wear anything but T-shirts and jeans. No one would notice if I put any effort into the way I look anyway. My wardrobe now is almost identical to Steve's, which is just plain sad. I do have some spectacular sun hats, though. More for practical purposes than anything else, but my mom used to say that an interesting hat says a lot about a person.

Storm has a subscription to both Italian and French *Vogue* and she practically camps out at the mailbox waiting for them. She reads them cover to cover and keeps me up to date on every new trend that I'm completely missing the boat on.

"Kelly bags are in this year," she'll inject into our conversation. "Chandelier earrings are all the rage for the holidays. Spike heels are out, stacked heels are back in," she'll announce, as though it's headline news.

She also likes to designer-name-drop. To Storm, knowing your designers is like knowing your state capitals. Names like Prada, and Versace, and Dolce and Gabbana, and Chanel are a drug to her. Just whispering them in her midst has been known to improve her mood considerably. Storm doesn't have the money for the real thing, so her outfits tend to be a bit Frankensteined together and I do give her high marks for creativity. When she cuts a matronly wool plaid skirt that she found at Goodwill into a miniskirt with a pair of sheers and shows me the same Burberry skirt in *Vogue* for nine hundred dollars, I tell her she's a genius.

My laissez-faire attitude toward fashion annoys Storm to no end, but then she's never so much as picked a flower out of a garden, so one cannot expect her to understand that Jimmy Choos are not the appropriate footwear for turning the compost heap or cleaning out the chicken coop.

Now that I've met Forest, I've started doing subtle things that I haven't thought about for a long time. The other day I changed my earrings, small gold hoops, for the first time in two years. I replaced them with a pair of turquoise drop earrings set in silver, a gift from Jane and Steve for my last birthday. Forest noticed right away. He also noticed when I exchanged a purple faded bandana for a blue one in my hair, and when I dabbed a bit of violet perfume on my wrists, it seemed to send him somewhere. I'm toying with pulling out the cowboy boots that Reynaldo and his wife had made for me by a friend of theirs in Mexico, which I wear very sparingly because they're a little on the fancy side. I keep them high up on the top shelf of my closet in their original box, wrapped up in tissue. There's a certain kind of girl you see quite a bit of around here who wears boots like that. These girls are a hot commodity on the rodeo scene and there are a lot of fringes and studs and rhinestones involved in their look. When the rodeo comes to town, they ride in the parade on the backs of spirited horses whose hooves have been spray-painted silver, or in Mustang convertibles driven by local Realtors wearing cowboy hats. They wave like the queen of England at the crowd lining the street, their heavily made-up faces frozen into a rictus for a smile. It's impossible to tell their age but you know that when they disappear there will always be someone fresh and young to take their place. A few of these rodeo-queens-in-training go to my high school but I don't know any of them personally. I don't register on their radar at all. I'm not descended from rodeo royalty and I'm not interested in the young sons of cattle ranchers that they seem to favor for boyfriend material. I'm neither a threat nor interesting enough for them to know, so they look past me. They don't know that I've taken hundreds of photos of them. Some of the photos of these girls are the best I've ever taken. They're the kind of photos that you always hold closer to your face so you can try to catch a glimpse of what's behind the mask.

I suppose that the reason I like taking photos of these girls is that I'm drawn to the idea of transformation, the idea of changing who you are. The appealing thing about putting on makeup and fancy clothes is that you get to be someone else for a while. I learned that from my mom. She was always transforming herself into someone else. Her ultimate transformation was becoming someone who wasn't a mother anymore. At least not mine.

13

$\mathcal{I}$ sit in the back of Forest's dad's rental car, inhaling new-car smell, while the unchanging landscape whizzes past my window. We've been driving for forty-five minutes because Forest's dad, the renowned Los Angeles psychiatrist Dr. Joshua Freidman, happened to ask a complete stranger on the street:

"Hey, where can a guy get some good Chinese food around here?"

We've already crossed one county line and we're about to cross another.

Forest was quick to tell me that Jews will cross a desert if they hear that there's good moo goo gai pan on the other side. I didn't know Forest was Jewish. Not that it matters. Actually he's half-Jewish. Driving in the car with these two makes me think of a line in a Paul Simon song that my mom used to love that goes:

One and one half wandering Jews,

free to wander wherever they choose,

Physically, Dr. Freidman is Forest in about twenty-five years. His hair is peppered with gray streaks and he wears glasses but he has the same sea-glass eyes. He's lean and much tanner than Forest. He seems very L.A. to me: He only goes one speed and all roads seem to lead to him.

Forest is very uncomfortable with me all the way in the backseat. I can tell because he keeps looking back apologetically. His dad is oblivious. It's obvious that he really loves Forest and he considers this time together precious. Dr. Freidman and Forest spent the afternoon at the hospital with Forest's mom. She'll be released tomorrow. Apparently, they make attempted suicides stay a couple of days for "observation." I'm guessing that it might not cheer her up much when she's served with a big fat lawsuit that says she's being sued for four hundred and fifty thousand dollars. I really hope Forest's theory is right.

I lean back and close my eyes, listening to Forest's conversation with his dad. They speak frankly and quietly and they don't hold anything back. Dr. Freidman's voice is even and measured, a psychiatrist's voice. The car radio is tuned to a classical music station, which plays so softly that I wonder if anyone but me can hear it.

"So is that putz still schtupping his receptionist?"

"I don't know. I don't think so. She kind of blew the whistle on him."

"Your mom deserves better. I hope she figures that out one day soon."

It's quiet for a few seconds.

"And don't look at me like that. It was different with us."

"How?"

"Well, for one thing I was honest with her."

"Yeah. That was really big of you."

"We were drifting apart. She knew it and I knew it. And, by the way, who got on a plane the next day when she was in trouble? You think that's easy for me?"

"No."

"You're damn right it's not. Your mother is a good person. She just happens to have a very low opinion of herself, and that particular personality trait attracts schmucks like bees to honey. I could kill that putz."

"Be careful. He's got a gun; I've seen it."

"He's got a gun? What in the hell does he need that for?"

"I dunno. Nothing, I guess. I've never even seen him take it out of its case."

"Then how do you know it's in there?"

"I checked. It's in there."

"Is it loaded?"

"I don't know. You think I know how to tell if a gun is loaded?"

"I don't like that. I don't like that at all. Maybe you should just come back to L.A. with me tomorrow."

My eyes fly open.

"Oh, sure, Dad. Becky would be thrilled."

Who's Becky?

"Becky adores you. I wish you could see that."

"Yeah. She adores me when I'm seven hundred miles away."

"Not true."

"Anyway. I want to be here for Mom. She needs me."

"What she needs is a good lawyer and a U-Haul to get the hell out of this god-forsaken place."

Forest looks back at me apologetically again and shrugs.

"Where the hell is this town?" says Dr. Freidman, as quietly as a person can say something like that. "Did we pass it? Have we gone nine miles on this road yet? God, I'm starving."

We finally come upon a sign for Lakeview and Dr. Freidman steers the car toward the off-ramp. We pull into the little town. It seems like an unlikely place for a Chinese restaurant but there it is, at the end of Main Street, a beacon in red neon letters that spells "Jade Palace." There will be no viewing of the lake in Lakeview today, if there even is one. Dr. Freidman is hungry and Chinese food is the only thing on his agenda. Judging by the number of cars parked out front, I'd say that we're onto something. Inside, the restaurant looks like every other Chinese restaurant I've ever been in. I think that when someone decides to open a Chinese restaurant, they order the "Chinese Restaurant in a Box," and a few days later, a large box arrives filled with black lacquer chairs, dusty-rose polyester tablecloths and matching napkins, an aquarium filled with tropical fish, Chinese prints for the walls, and a few Chinese lanterns. You just pull everything out of the box and hang up the "Open" sign.

Dr. Freidman is undaunted by the way the place looks. He acts as though we've discovered the Holy Grail. He seems energized by the fact that a lot of the tables are filled with happy diners. He greets the hostess as though she were a long-lost friend, showing more emotion than he did on the entire car ride. He follows her to a table. Forest and I trail behind. I try to smooth the wrinkles out of my linen skirt but it's hopeless.

Forest rolls his eyes at me. "The Jews and Chinese restaurants have an affiliation based on the fact that the Chinese restaurants are always open when the Jews are hungry, particularly on Christian holidays, like Christmas."

"This place is pretty popular," says Dr. Freidman as his

new best friend hands him a menu.

Before I even get a chance to spread my dusty-rose napkin onto my lap, he starts firing questions at the waiter, who's just arrived at our table.

"Are the clams fresh?"

"Yes, very fresh." He nods.

"What about the lobster? Is it Maine or Pacific?"

"Maine. We have local Dungeness crab too. Very good, wok charred with ginger and scallion sauce."

"Can we get some tea?"

"Right away."

The waiter disappears and Dr. Freidman finally addresses me.

"Roar, what do you like to eat?"

"Well, I eat fish, but no meat or shellfish for me."

He looks annoyed. He was thinking he had a recruit for his all-star eating team and I've been exposed as a tofu-eater. "Okay, so she eats *nothing*," he says quietly, perusing the menu some more.

"Dad, she eats great. A lot better than you and me."

He's not interested.

The waiter returns and Dr. Freidman turns ordering Chinese food into an art form. I sit back and watch in awe. He's deconstructed the menu and come up with a combination of food that even the chef will be awestruck by, and if seventeen people were joining us it would actually make sense.

"Dad, that's too much food," Forest says as the waiter disappears.

"No, it's not. I'm very hungry and we can take it home."

"You're leaving tomorrow morning."

"I might get hungry later. I'll take it to the hotel."

"Where are you staying?" I ask.

"Some sort of B and B in a farmhouse, Peggy's or Penny's or something like that."

"Polly's?" I offer.

"That's it, Polly's."

The tea arrives and he sips from his tiny cup.

"Do you like it?"

"The tea?"

"No, Polly's."

"Yeah, sure, it's okay. Noisy, though. I had to sleep with earplugs. They get up at five a.m. and start banging things around and then the rooster starts crowing and the dogs start barking. It's not exactly restful, you know?"

Apparently, the charm of a farmhouse bed-and-breakfast is lost on Dr. Freidman.

Although he's polite to me, I quickly discover that this time together is exclusively for him and his son, and the only time I'm invited into the conversation is when Forest negotiates it. I imagine that Dr. Freidman isn't especially keen on the idea of his son falling in love with a farm girl. Someone who, at first glance, looks like she could convince him to forsake his dream of becoming a writer and settle down on a dirt farm and raise freckled, snotty-nosed kids, while living near the poverty line. To him, I am an interloper, a bump in the road that should probably be steered clear of. He doesn't know who I really am, but I think he might find out soon, and I cringe when I imagine what he'll think of me then. He does turn to me at one point and ask me why I walk around with a camera around my neck. I tell him it's because I like to take pictures. He seems satisfied with that answer and doesn't pursue it any further.

Our food starts to arrive on great glistening platters. A whole fish that looks like it's still swimming in the ocean is placed directly in front of me. It watches me accusingly. I shift the platter away from me. Dr. Freidman digs in with gusto. Forest passes me the food that he knows I'll eat and it is quite good. Back when I lived in the city, we ate at a tiny Chinese place in our neighborhood called Yuet Lee. It had fluorescent green walls. That place was better, but this isn't bad for the middle of nowhere. When we're finished eating, there's enough food left over to end world hunger. It's boxed up for us and placed on our table. We look like we're catering a wedding later. The fortune cookies arrive and Dr. Freidman pulls his apart and reads the contents aloud.

" 'You will find your correct path soon.' " He laughs. "Well, I found this place okay."

Mine says, "Beware of trouble ahead," and Forest's says, "Take time to enjoy the small things." I never eat a fortune cookie without trying to imagine the person who sits there all day writing these pearls of wisdom. Is this person even Chinese, or do the cookie makers just buy fortunes by the bagful from a salesman named Bernie who sells restaurant supplies? I remember when I was a little girl I took my fortunes very seriously, thinking that they were a direct line to some sort of eastern mysticism. I would carry them around with me for months until they disintegrated or went through the wash and disappeared.

On the drive home, I sit in the backseat again and watch the sun disappear out of the sky. The odor of congealing Chinese food seeps into the car from the trunk. Dr. Freidman and Forest continue their conversation and it occurs to me that they may not get a lot of alone time back in L.A., with Becky hanging around. Judging by the number of times she called him on his cell phone in the last three hours, I would say that she's pretty high maintenance. Dr. Freidman's tone with her on the phone is patient and consoling. He speaks to her the way you would speak to a distraught nine-year-old. Forest told me that she's almost half his dad's age.

I let my eyes close.

Dr. Freidman drops us in the hospital parking lot, where Forest's car is parked. Forest picked me up at the tar pits earlier and his dad stayed at the hospital. There is much affectionate hugging as Dr. Freidman says good-bye to his son. Back in Forest's car, sitting next to him, I feel as though we've suddenly morphed from children into grown-ups.

"Well, that was an unmitigated disaster," says Forest, taking my hand as he navigates the country road.

"Don't worry about it. I'm fine. It was actually kind of fun."

"Fun? Don't humor me."

I squeeze his hand.

"Man, I sure wish I didn't have to go home tonight. I wish I could stay with you."

I look out the window at the darkness. The moon is almost full. "It's early. My dad thinks I'm out with Storm. We could take a walk if you like."

"Okay. Where to?"

"There's a road I know of that goes through the cornfields. It's really cool at night when the moon is full. You don't even need a flashlight. Keep going up to the stop sign and take a right."

We park the car in a ditch and I find the road easily. It's wide enough for farm machinery to pass so there's no chance of getting lost. We walk along in the moonlight, holding hands. I get the feeling that Forest wants to tell me something.

"You look really beautiful tonight. I've never seen you in a skirt before."

"I didn't want to look like a farm girl but I don't think your dad noticed."

"Oh, he noticed, all right."

The road is enclosed on both sides with endless identical six-foot cornstalks. It's the kind of thing you see in bad horror films where a crazy person who's supposed to be dead jumps out of the darkness with a bloody ax, and the girl in short shorts, carrying an unreliable flashlight, shrieks and tries to run away, but somehow the slow-moving murderer always catches her.

We walk without speaking till I can't stand it anymore.

"You're not going to leave early, are you?" I ask tentatively.

"No way. I'm staying."

"Where will you go after you finish high school in L.A.?"

"I'm applying to NYU. Didn't I tell you that?"

"No." I feel foolish for thinking he would hide that from me.

"I want to get into the writing program."

"That's great."

He sighs heavily. "Yeah."

"Why the heavy sigh?"

He thinks for a moment. "Is it crazy to think that we'll still be together when I go to school?"

"No. It's not crazy."

"Because when I think of myself in New York, I think about you there with me. I think about us together."

"That's really nice." *Really nice? It's incredible!*

Forest smiles at me with a little uncertainty in his eyes.

"And when you visualize us in New York together, what are we wearing?"

"Scarves and heavy sweaters and we're walking through Central Park. You have your camera and I'm carrying a stack of books."

"That does sound nice."

"Yeah. Woody Allen directed it."

We walk along quietly again for a minute and then I see a light through the cornstalks. Forest notices it too. It looks like a small campfire. The breeze suddenly smells like roasted meat. We hear voices speaking Spanish. We continue on, and through the corn we see a small encampment tucked into a circle that's been cleared of cornstalks. Three Hispanic farmworkers sit around the fire talking. They haven't seen us. Latin salsa music plays on a small radio leaning against a rock. A small lean-to is set up behind them. I motion to Forest that we should turn around before they see us. We walk back the way we came.

"What was that?" asks Forest, when we're far enough down the road.

"An encampment. They're everywhere. Workers who can't afford accommodation camp out wherever they can find a spot."

"So that's where they live?"

"No, that's where they sleep. They live in Mexico. All their money gets sent home to their families and they don't want to spend any more than they have to on a place to live."

"Wow, Tomás and Miguel are lucky."

I look at him.

"God, I can't believe I said that. I am such an idiot."

"Never mind. I know what you meant."

We're not ready to go home so we lay on the hood of Forest's car, looking up at the sky. It's a clear night and the inky sky is spattered with stars. I make a wish on the first star I see. I feel incredibly lucky tonight. Forest and I sing every song we can think of with the word "star" in it, starting with "Twinkle, Twinkle Little Star" and moving on to David Bowie's "Space Oddity" and "The Prettiest Star" and Madonna's "Lucky Star." There's really no turning back once you've sung the lyrics to a Madonna song badly on the hood of a car that's parked in a ditch and lit by the moon.

14

$\mathcal{T}$he next morning, after I let the unappreciative chickens out of their coop and collect their eggs, I wander down to the road to get the coffee-can money from the farm stand and pick up yesterday's mail. The late July heat has arrived in full force and sweat trickles down the back of my neck. I pull up my heavy hair and let the hot breeze tickle my damp skin.

I shake the coffee can and pull off the plastic lid. There's twenty-seven dollars and seventy-five cents in it. I stuff the money into my pocket. The garlic is all gone and we need more bunches of onions and baskets of potatoes. I make a mental note. As I put the lid back on the can I see a white piece of paper stuck to the bottom of the can. I pull it out and unfold it. In what looks like a child's handwriting it says: *DROP THE LAWSUIT NOW, OR THERE WILL*

BE TROUBLE. I read it again, trying to make sense of it. I look up and down the empty road. My scalp gets all prickly.

My dad is working at the kitchen table when I deliver the coffee-can threat to him. He has a fan set up on the kitchen counter and it oscillates back and forth, blowing his papers whenever it comes around. He's using large tomatoes for paperweights.

"It's probably the farmworkers," he says, holding the folded slip of paper in front of him. "They're afraid that this lawsuit will bring unwanted attention to them."

"C'mon, Dad. Look at it again. Not one mistake. That note was written by someone who speaks English."

"Maybe, maybe not. Lots of the workers speak fluent English."

"Well, if it is them, they've got a point, don't you think?"

"Depends on how you look at it. If Tomás wins, it's a victory for all undocumented workers. They don't do themselves any favors by staying invisible. They need a voice. People need to know that they're here to stay and that we couldn't survive without them."

"And if he loses?"

My dad shrugs.

"If he loses he could get deported, couldn't he?"

"It's possible. But that's always a possibility. Even

162

without the lawsuit." My dad looks down at the floor. "Tomás knows the risks. I was clear about them. I'll do whatever I can to keep him in the country. Don't you think he deserves some compensation for what happened?"

I don't answer that. "Are you using Tomás to make a statement?"

"Of course not. I'm just helping Tomás access what he's entitled to. You know that."

"What did Reynaldo tell you to do?" I ask.

"Reynaldo is coming from a different place. He doesn't want the grape pickers to be afraid to cross the border. He wants a better life for the farmworkers but he doesn't want to risk anything. You can't make change without stirring things up."

"So he was against it."

"Yes."

"Don't make Tomás your sacrificial lamb just to prove a point, Dad. That's not fair."

"Have some faith, Roar. Ned's a damn good lawyer. He's the first guy I'd call if I was in trouble."

"You *are* in trouble. Someone just threatened you."

My dad looks me in the eye. "Do you think I'd be scared off that easily?"

It seems that no matter what I think or how torn I am about it, this machine has been set in motion. I look at my dad with his head bent over his work again, his jaw set, like it always is, with determination. I do have faith in him and in Uncle Ned too. I just hope they're doing the right thing. I hope that no one gets hurt or even killed before all of this is over. Losing Sylvia was enough.

I flip through the big pile of mail that I just set down on the kitchen table next to the crumpled coffee-can money. Underneath a stack of flyers advertising things we never buy rests a big glossy photography magazine called *FOTO*. It's addressed to me but I didn't order it or pay for it. The first time it showed up, I thought it was a free trial offer or something, but it showed up again the next month and now here it is again. It's published in New York and it's filled with cutting-edge photos taken by dark, brooding photographers with names like Freundlich and Gustav. It also features articles on the art of taking photos, developing techniques, and reviews on new equipment. The back pages of the magazine are filled with ads for esteemed East Coast photography schools and announcements for photography exhibits at chic galleries in Soho and Chelsea. I flip through it quickly. I'm about to close it when something catches my eye: It's an ad for a photography contest, nondigital only. I skip the rules and go right to the prize. It's ten thousand dollars. I carry the magazine up to my room and close the door.

I've never entered my work in a contest before. This one seems pretty straightforward. You can submit up to three photos in the color category and the same for black-and-white. The contest closes in mid-August and the entry fee is twenty dollars. I get on my computer and go to the website that has the entry form. I download it and print it out. I fill in my name, address, and phone number. When I come to the part where you're supposed to fill in your age, I stop, think about it, and write twenty-one.

It takes me an agonizing hour to choose the photos I'll send in. After spreading out all my best work into categories on my bed and eliminating anything I'm not wild about, I still can't see my quilt through all the photos. I finally narrow it down to six. For the three color photos I settle on a series from the Buddhist monastery. Two of them are the monks working in the garden, and one of them is a young smiling monk eating a pink radish. The composition is good and the colors are brilliant. For black-and-white, I choose a series from the rodeo parade. One rodeo queen, one rodeo clown who looks like he'd rather be anywhere else, and a tiny highland dancer in a kilt and kneesocks and bouncing ringlets, frowning as she concentrates on her dance steps. I put the photos between cardboard and put them in my backpack with the completed entry form.

On a whim, I open the magazine to the inside cover

and find the 1-800 number to call for subscriptions. I find the phone and dial.

"National Magazine Distribution, can I help you?" Clearly I'm not calling New York; this woman has a southern accent as thick as pancake batter.

"Hi, um. I have a magazine subscription that I got as a gift and I was wondering if I could find out who sent it to me."

"What's your name, hon?"

"Aurora Audley."

"Can you spell that?"

I spell it and I hear the clicking of a computer keyboard. She asks for my zip code.

"Is it *FOTO* magazine?"

"Yes."

"Well, the gift was anonymous but the bill went to Key West, Florida. I probably shouldn't even be telling you that."

"Thank you. I appreciate it."

"You have a nice day now."

I hang up the phone.

Key West, Florida? I don't know even one person in the entire state of Florida. Who could have sent this to me and why?

I look at my bedside clock. Storm is picking me up

in half an hour. I'll get her to stop at the post office so I can buy a money order and an envelope for my photos. I take a twenty-dollar bill out of a jewelry box that I keep my work money in and stuff it in the front pocket of my backpack.

I spoke to Forest this morning while my dad was outside. He said that his mom seemed to be doing better. She'd been served with the papers earlier and it was like she'd been expecting them. She calmly called her insurance company and read them the details over the phone. After that she called a locksmith and asked him to come over and change the locks on the doors, and then she called a divorce lawyer, the same one she'd used when she and his dad divorced. After she discussed filing for divorce with her lawyer, she called Jerry's cell phone and left a message that all of his belongings would be on the front porch by five p.m. and he could pick them up anytime after that. Then she poured herself a cup of coffee and sat down at the kitchen table to read the newspaper.

It appears that Connie Gilwood has a new outlook.

I hear Storm's scooter as I'm digging through a pile of clothes looking for something clean to wear. I settle on sort of clean cutoffs and a wrinkled tank top that used to be a T-shirt until I cut off the sleeves. I slip into my clogs and grab my backpack. In the unlikely event that my dad actually talks to Storm, I don't want the conversation getting around to all the fun things we've been doing lately that we actually haven't. Storm isn't good at the small details.

By the time I get outside, Storm is already engaged in her ongoing flirtation with Steve. She has him bent over looking at the tires of her scooter as she gives him a full-on view of her cleavage emerging from a pale blue halter top. Her hair is loosely piled on her head and she's wearing short shorts and espadrilles with stacked four-inch heels. Her legs look nine feet long.

"I think you're fine, I don't see anything." Steve stands up, wiping his hands on his pants.

"Hey, Roar, I was just telling Steve here how I hit a rock on the way over and I was worried I might have punctured a tire. He was nice enough to take a look." She says it in her sultry "boys only" voice, smiling at Steve.

A look at what? Your breasts?

I smirk at Steve, who smirks back. I get on Storm's scooter behind her.

At Millie's I watch Storm rip the tops off three packs of sugar and pour them into her coffee.

"So, Doo-wayne is history," she says, stirring her coffee.

"Doo-wayne?"

"Yeah, the cowboy. Man, what an idiot. I left that stupid gold horseshoe necklace in the ashtray of his truck. It was turning my neck green."

I notice that today she's wearing a gold chain with a cameo pendant hanging on it, another family jewel "borrowed" from her mom's jewelry box.

"Why the change of heart?"

"Well, as I mentioned before, he's an idiot."

"Can you be a bit more specific?"

"Turns out he has a girlfriend in Stockton and a BABY! Can you believe that?"

"No!" I do my soap-opera shocked face. "How'd you find out?"

"He opens his wallet to pay for our drinks and there's a picture of the happy couple with a newborn baby, one of those cheap photos too, that you do at the Sears Portrait Studio. What the hell was I thinking?"

"Did you ask him about it?"

"Of course I asked him about it. He actually tried to tell me that it was his twin brother."

"Are you sure it's not?"

"Twin brothers with the same tattoos and the same scar above the same eye?"

"Okay, well, it's good that you found out sooner than later, right?"

"Yeah, I guess. I did spray all his stupid cowboy shirts with my perfume, though. He can wash them fifty times and they'll still smell like me. Here's the really funny part. The perfume is called Envy."

One thing I'll say for Storm: She's never boring.

Millie comes over to take our order. I get the usual: grilled cheese sandwich with tomato slices that we most likely grew, and home fries. Storm gets a cheeseburger.

As Millie's writing everything down she asks me if I've seen today's paper.

"Which one?"

"The *Gazette*."

The *Gazette* is a local rag that I rarely read because it's gossipy and written by hacks who have no business attempting journalism.

"No, why?"

"I think you should have a look." She disappears for a few seconds and comes back with a thin newspaper, which she lays in front of me. The headline reads:

MEXICAN FARMWORKER SUES LOCAL WOMAN FOR WRONGFUL DEATH

Storm leans forward and reads it upside down. "Don't worry, hardly anyone reads the paper around here."

Millie is still standing there, waiting for my reaction.

I shrug. "So what?"

She sucks in her breath. "This town is in for some interesting times and I, for one, can't wait." She looks like a kid who's excited about the circus coming to town.

"Millie, can I get some more coffee?" asks Storm.

Millie reluctantly goes to find the coffeepot.

"It's kind of sexy the way your dad likes to stir things up around here," says Storm, taking a wad of gum out of her mouth and wrapping it in a napkin.

"Shut up!" I skim the article. They quote Uncle Ned: "Tomás Rodriguez has every right to pursue compensation. I'm proud to represent him. It's a landmark case for social justice."

God, he sounds like Che Guevara. I fold up the newspaper and put it in my backpack. I don't want to think about this anymore. It's starting to make my stomach hurt.

"So, did you tell Forest about how you're helping send his mom to the electric chair?"

"It's a civil suit. It's about money, not punishment."

"So, did you tell him?"

"No. I didn't."

Millie reappears with a coffeepot and fills our cups.

"Honey, you tell your dad to watch his back. A lot of folks around this place don't take too kindly to things being stirred up."

"Yeah, like who?" I think about the coffee-can note.

"Well, Brody Burk, for one."

"My dad's not afraid of Brody Burk."

Storm suddenly joins in. "He should be. Brody's got goons. Those idiots will do whatever he says. They once took one of Brody's dogs and threw it out of a moving truck because it wasn't any good at hunting."

"My dad's not afraid." I feel my jaw clenching.

Millie smiles at me sympathetically like maybe she understands that it might be tough being the daughter of a person like that. "Honey, everyone's a little bit afraid of Brody Burk."

After we leave Millie's, Storm and I walk up the street to the post office, which is the unofficial pickup spot for casual farm labor, so there are always a lot of Hispanic men standing around watching for pickup trucks. This is also the place where they come to convert their paychecks into money orders so that they can send them home to their families. I've always been invisible to these men but today I get a weird vibe from them. I don't think they're looking at Storm's nine-foot-long legs, I think they're looking at me. It appears that the word is out among the farmworkers. And maybe I'm a little paranoid but the locals we pass along the way all seem to be carrying the *Gazette*, reading the *Gazette*, or buying the *Gazette*. I guess Storm was just trying to make me feel better. I had no idea that it was such a popular paper. I always assumed that people around here read the *San Francisco Chronicle* or the *New York Times*. I thought that small-town living would make you crave national news. I couldn't have been more wrong about that. These people don't want to know what's going on in the world. *This* is their world.

15

*T*he law offices of Funk, McIntyre, and Monk, where Connie Gilwood's lawyers will be interviewing me, is located in a beige plaza occupied by other lawyers' and dentists' and doctors' offices, generally a group of professionals that people dread visiting. It's about ninety degrees outside and the oak-paneled boardroom that the receptionist escorts us to is as chilly as a meat locker. It feels nice for about thirty seconds and then my teeth start to chatter. It must be some sort of intimidation device. My dad and I sit down in giant leatherette chairs that are gathered around a massive oak conference table. The outside wall of the boardroom is made of glass and you can actually watch the farms disappear from here as the developers take over a few hundred acres at a time and turn them into "communities" and strip malls. There isn't much to do as we wait for the lawyers except listen to the receptionist, back at her desk, repeat, "Good afternoon, Funk, McIntyre, and Monk," over and over again.

I'm wearing a clean white blouse with short sleeves, and my linen skirt and sandals. I showered this morning, but the air-conditioning in my dad's truck has never worked so I already feel grimy and rumpled, but I don't care. I just want this over with. My dad is wearing his work clothes (but they're clean) and a big fat "don't mess with me" look on his face.

After a couple of minutes, two men in matching serious suits enter the boardroom. A woman, a court reporter, devoid of all facial expression, follows behind them and sets up her little machine in the corner. Her suit is the color of concrete. The men introduce themselves to my dad. One of them is Monk, the other one is named Johnson. His suit is a better fit and quality than Monk's. I'm guessing he's in from the big firm in the city. The big gun sent in to keep the damages to a minimum. My dad introduces me. Monk sizes me up and his "cool as a cucumber" expression vanishes. Johnson's expression is unreadable. He's better at this. On the drive over, my dad told me this might happen. I'm what they call a "grade-A" witness. I'm young and bright and fresh and I look like I tell the truth. If this case goes to trial and I walk into a courtroom and tell the jury what happened that day, they will hang on my every word. And no matter what I tell them, they will believe me. The insurance company wouldn't have a prayer. The lawyers exchange a look. I know what this look means. It means that this case cannot go to trial.

Uncle Ned rushes into the room at the last second. He's dressed as a lawyer too. There's not a trace of banjo player on him anywhere. He's carrying a leather briefcase and he shakes hands with the grim twins and squeezes my shoulder as he sits down next to me at the boardroom table. He leans across the table and shakes my dad's hand as though they're just casual acquaintances and not old friends. I feel as though everyone in this room is pretending to be someone they're not. To everyone here, I look like a person who isn't capable of telling a lie, but in the last few weeks I've told so many lies that I've lost count. Even my being here is a big lie because somehow I never got around to telling Forest about it. Somehow the right moment never arrived.

Johnson trains a small video camera on me and loads a tape. Then I take an oath to tell the truth, the whole truth, and nothing but the truth, so help me God.

Johnson sits across from me and rifles through a stack of papers. He looks up at me and smiles like the Cat in the Hat. It appears that he'll be asking the questions and Monk will watch and learn.

"Aurora. Can you tell me about the morning of the accident, starting with the moment that you got into the vehicle with your dad?"

"Okay. Well. It was about six a.m. . . ."

"About six a.m.? Can you be more exact?"

"It was six a.m. We got in the truck and my dad started driving down Orchard Road toward the freeway."

"Was it daylight?"

"Yes."

"Was the weather clear?"

"Yes."

"Continue."

"I started to doze off."

Johnson and Monk exchange looks.

"I woke up a few minutes later because my dad was looking in his rearview mirror and yelling."

"What was he yelling, Aurora?"

I look over at my dad. His eyes narrow. I know he can't remember what he was yelling. Uncle Ned is scribbling notes.

"He was yelling 'Goddamn development people!'"

"How do you suppose he knew it was a development person in the vehicle?"

"They're always in a hurry like that."

"So, he was yelling because the driver of the car behind you was in a hurry?"

"No, the SUV was right behind us, right on our bumper, and she . . ."

"She? You could tell it was a woman driving?"

"Sure. She was right behind us."

"Okay. Continue."

"She was honking her horn. I think she wanted us to let her pass but there's no shoulder there, you can't pull over."

Johnson and Uncle Ned take notes furiously.

"We came to the part of the road that runs straight for a while but you're still not allowed to pass there. The lines are solid yellow."

"The lines were solid yellow? You're sure?" asks Johnson.

"Yes."

"You seem to know a lot about driving, Aurora. Have you ever driven a car yourself?"

I swallow. "Uh, no," I answer, not a lie. I've driven a Jeep, not a car.

"You've never driven? You live on a farm. You must have driven something, a tractor, perhaps?"

My dad is watching me with interest.

"Uh . . ." I remember that I'm under oath. "Yeah, sure. I've driven a tractor and . . . a Jeep."

"A Jeep. On the highway?"

"Uh, yes."

My dad's eyebrows go up. My first, in a long list of lies, is exposed. I know I'm going to hear about this later.

Johnson makes a note. "Okay, so you know a bit about the rules of the road." Monk grimaces. Not only am I a star witness but, at fifteen, I have driving experience.

"Let's continue with what happened that morning. You came to the part where you're not allowed to pass. . . . "

"And the woman pulled out from behind us and started to pass us. When she got up to my dad's window she slowed down for a few seconds and gave him the finger. She took her eyes off the road and looked right at him."

"Can you show us the, uh, gesture? You know, with your own hand?"

"Sure." I give him the finger. My dad and Uncle Ned grin and look away.

"Okay." Johnson reddens slightly. "Let the record show that Miss Audley is holding up the middle finger on her right hand. Continue."

"The straightaway ends there and the road dips down into a little valley. The pickup came around the corner in the oncoming lane and the SUV couldn't get out of the way in time and she smashed into the right half of the front bumper. The pickup spun around and flipped over the edge into the ravine and the SUV continued on for a few hundred feet and tipped over in the middle of the road."

"Was the pickup driving in its own lane?"

"Yes. She tried to pull off to the right when she saw the SUV but there was nowhere to go."

"And who called 9-1-1?"

"I did."

"And why you and not your dad?"

"He told me to. He jumped out of the truck and ran to help Sylvia."

"Sylvia. The woman driving the pickup?"

"Yes."

"And was your dad able to help Mrs. Rodriguez?"

"Well, no. Sylvia was trapped. But he took the baby, Rosa, out of her car seat. And carried her out of the ravine and gave her to me. Then he went back to Sylvia. He talked to her until the paramedics came."

"And did your dad try to help the SUV driver?"

"No."

"Was Mrs. Rodriguez alive when they pulled her out of the pickup?"

My eyes fill with tears. "Yes. I think so. But she looked really bad. Her arm was crushed. She was losing a lot of blood." I wipe my eyes on the back of my hand and Uncle

Ned hands me a tissue. The court reporter gets a tiny wrinkle between her eyes but she keeps tapping away.

Monk and Johnson exchange grim looks.

"Did you get a good look at the pickup after the accident?"

"Yes. Actually I have photos of it."

"You took photos?" Johnson's eyes widen slightly.

"Yes."

"How did you think to take photos during all of this?"

"I take photos of everything. I'm a photographer."

"A photographer."

"Yes."

"You have photos of both cars at the accident scene?"

"Yes."

Johnson's and Monk's eyes meet again.

"So, Aurora, to your knowledge, no one else saw the accident?"

I shake my head. "No."

"Okay, Aurora. I just have one more question and I want you to think about this very carefully. If Connie Gilwood, the woman driving the SUV, hadn't slowed alongside your dad's truck to deliver that, um, gesture, do you think she still would have hit the pickup?"

I try to relive that moment but it's just impossible to remember something in split seconds when it all seemed to happen in slow motion. "I don't know. Maybe."

"Thank you, Aurora. That's all we need from you today."

Everyone in the room seems to exhale. Uncle Ned gives me a discreet thumbs-up and my dad comes around the table and hugs me. I think now would be a good time to tell him that it was me who backed the tractor into the side of the barn in May and not Steve.

On the way home in the truck my dad tells me that he thought it went really well. I wait for him to mention the fact that I've been driving without his permission but he says nothing.

"You're a star. You were fantastic. There's no way they're going to put you on the stand. I'm confident that they'll try to settle."

"On TV the star witness always turns up dead."

"That's just TV crap."

"I hope that this is all over soon. Do you think the insurance company will pay?"

"Insurance companies are slippery. They'll try all kinds of tricks to weasel out of paying. They might appeal it but I don't see how they have too many options here. Connie hired her own lawyer too, which is smart. She's going to need one."

I wonder for a second why he called her Connie and

not Connie Gilwood like he usually does. It seems a little familiar for someone he's never really met. I suddenly feel an overwhelming need to talk to Forest. I want to tell him everything that happened today and have him assure me in his quiet way that it's all going to be okay. As we drive through town, I look for his car on the off chance that maybe he's here. I would feel so much better if I could just catch a glimpse of his face. I don't see his car anywhere. I look in the window of Millie's but there's no one sitting in the booths. It's the kind of hot where no one feels like eating and coffee is out of the question.

When I get home, I climb the stairs up to my room. My legs feel like lead. My bedroom is as hot as it ever gets, even with the oak tree shading the roof. My windows are wide-open but the curtains stay dead still. I turn a fan on high and pull off my sticky clothes. I stand in front of it naked and let the breeze cool my skin before I pull on my cutoffs and a tank top. Rufus has disappeared to the coolest corner of the barn. He'll stay there till he's hungry and then he'll emerge covered in straw, looking sheepish because he knows he's neglected his guard dog duties.

I sit down in front of my computer and open my mail. There's an email from Forest. It was written half an hour ago.

To: Photogirl@earthlink.net
From: Hamonrye@yahoo.com
Re: Miss u

Roar,

Where have U been? I'm dying to see U. Can U meet
me later? I've been thinking about your chin all day, your
lovely, lovely chin. Call if U can.

Yours 4-ever,

4-est

Ever since I told Forest that I hate email abbreviations,
he includes them in all his letters. I run my finger along my
chin, trying to figure out what's so lovely about it.

I can hear my dad on the phone downstairs in the
kitchen. He's all fired up about the deposition. I think he
must be talking to Uncle Ned. He'll probably be on the
phone forever so I send Forest an email telling him to meet
me at the tar pits in an hour. I pull off my clothes again and
put my bathing suit on and put them back on over it. I load
up my backpack with a bottle of water that I fill from the
pitcher in the fridge with chunks of ice in it. I also grab a
plastic container of Ambrosia melon chunks and two plums
from a bowl sitting on the table in front of my dad. He
winks at me. Since the deposition I've been elevated from

"daughter" to "secret weapon," kind of like the pen that shoots poison darts in a Bond movie. I find a sort of clean towel in the laundry room and go back upstairs and click my email on again. Forest has responded:

> Roar.
> I'll B there.
> F.

I'm bumping along on the narrow dirt road when a black truck passes me slowly. I recognize it from the pit bull in the back. The truck slows and stops about fifty feet ahead of me diagonally, blocking my way. I stop pedaling. Brody Burk eases himself out of the driver's side and walks around to the back of the truck. He leans up against the tailgate and watches me.

"Afternoon, miss," he says, slightly lowering the brim of his black hat. There's a sweat stain along the hatband. His hat is meant for winter. No one around here wears a felt hat in the summer heat. I see that he also has sweat stains in the armpits of his fancy western shirt.

I don't respond. There's no room for me to pass on the right and I don't like the look on his dog's face so I start to squeeze my bike to the left of the truck. Suddenly Brody lunges at my handlebars and hangs on. I skid to a stop. He grins at me. The dog growls.

"I wonder if I could have a moment of your time," he says with a Texas drawl, even though he was born right here.

My heart is thundering. I watch his big hand on my handlebars, holding tight. His other hand casually twirls a toothpick in his mouth.

"Ya know, this thing your dad is doin', this campaign to save those dirty Mexicans, I'd really hate to see someone hurt along the way, or worse . . . dead, wouldn't you?" He says the last part slowly with the emphasis on the word "dead." I smell alcohol on his breath.

I say nothing.

"Because, ya know, when you think about it, if those Mexicans weren't here in the first place, well, none of this woulda happened now, would it?"

I still don't respond. I try to force my face into something that doesn't look as scared as I feel. He takes his hand off my handlebars and grabs onto my upper arm. I look down at his fingernails, which are clean, betraying his cowboy image. He squeezes hard and I pull back. He hangs on tighter. He's hurting me.

"You seem like a nice girl. Maybe you could convince your dad to leave this alone. Not much point in it anyway, ain't gonna be no farms left around here soon, and then all them criminals can head back to that shithole of a country they came from." He lets go of my arm and touches the brim of his hat. "You think you could do that for me, sugar? You think you could talk to him? Why don't ya try?" He winks.

I start to pedal away from him; my legs are shaking. The pit bull lunges at me, barking. I almost shriek in fear.

"You have yourself a nice day now, ya hear?" he calls after me.

I arrive at the tar pits ahead of Forest, gasping and hot and terrified. I'm completely nauseous and I'm not sure I won't throw up right there. I drop my bike and sit down in the shade of a live oak, taking deep breaths, trying to calm myself. It's too hot to stay onshore. I yank off my clothes and wade into the greenish cool water. It calms my hot skin. I spread my arms out and float on my back, looking up at the sky, trying to banish Brody's leering face from my mind. A few minutes pass and I hear Forest's car. I tread water as he turns off the noisy engine and all is still again except for the gentle sloshing of water against the muddy bank. He pulls off his clothes and leaves them in a pile next to mine. He's wearing swim trunks that could possibly be considered retro in L.A., but around here people would point and laugh. He wades into the water and swims out to me. He immediately sees that I'm upset.

"What? You're shaking. What happened?"

I tell him. I show him the mark on my arm, the outline

of Brody's fingers. He puts out his arms and pulls me to him and we stay like that for a while, our legs moving just enough to keep us above water.

"I have to tell you something else too," I say.

"Tell me." His face is inches from mine. I feel exposed. I try not to cry.

"I went to a deposition today. I had to tell them what happened that day."

"I know."

"You know?"

"Yeah. My mom's lawyer told her and she told me. She calls you 'that farm girl.'"

"Wait, how long have you known?"

"A while."

"Why didn't you say something?"

"I figured you'd tell me when you were ready."

I stare at him. Could someone possibly be this cool? Could I be this lucky? I kiss him softly and pull away, studying his face. His long eyelashes are wet and it makes his eyes look bluer and greener. He has more color in his face than when he first arrived, especially on his nose and his forehead and his chin.

"Now, I have to tell you something," he says.

"Tell me."

"I love you."

"How long have you known?"

"A long time."

"Why are you telling me now?"

"Because, I need you to know."

Being loved by someone who isn't your parent, someone who wanders into your life and slowly comes to know you and understand you, is sort of like being reborn. You walk around knowing that under his gaze, you are lovable, desirable, interesting, funny, and beautiful. No one has ever looked at me like this before. No one has ever made me feel this way with just a few words or a glance or a touch. The whole concept of two people falling in love like in the movies or on TV has always seemed so stupid to me. I'd roll my eyes and look away. But this thing I have with Forest is much more than TV love. It feels real. I love the way I feel knowing that someone is thinking about me this way. It makes me see myself in a whole new way.

I'm too afraid to tell him I love him back. I'm afraid he'll think that I think I should. So I don't. But I do love him. And I know that he'll wait patiently for it like he does everything else.

That night I can't sleep. The cool night air never arrives and I lay on top of my quilt spread-eagle with the fan blowing on me. I can't stop thinking about Brody. I can't stop thinking about what Forest told me today. Everything has me stirred up and I'm scared and giddy and restless. When I got home from the tar pits, I told my dad what happened. He cursed Brody Burk and called him an ignorant bully. Then he hugged me for a while and said how sorry he was that he dragged me into all of this. I already knew that he wouldn't back down, though; I know my dad. He doesn't respond to threats.

I hear a car in the driveway and check my clock. It's almost midnight. As the sound of the car comes closer, red and blue lights start to revolve around my room. I hear the jumbled static of a police radio. I jump out of bed and look out my open window. A police officer is walking up to the house. Rufus is barking at him. My dad is already on the staircase. I hear the whine of the screen door and then I hear him talking to the cop. His tone of voice changes from fear to anger. I keep watching at the window as my dad and the cop walk over to the patrol car. The cop opens the back passenger door and roughly pulls Miguel out as though he's a criminal. He undoes his plastic handcuffs. Miguel rubs his wrists and he and my dad speak quickly to each other in Spanish. The cop goes around to the other side and gets Tomás out. Even from my window, I can tell that Tomás has been beaten. One of his eyes is almost shut and he's bleeding from a cut on his cheek. There's blood all over the front of his white T-shirt. The cop releases his handcuffs and my dad speaks to Tomás in Spanish. Tomás shakes his head and looks down at the ground. My dad asks the cop why he handcuffed them if they weren't under arrest. The cop says they were involved in a bar fight and they were being "uncooperative." My dad asks Miguel if that's true and Miguel shakes his head no and explains something to my dad.

"He says he couldn't understand you. He doesn't speak English," my dad says to the cop.

"Well, he should learn. This is the United Sates of America. We speak English here. This is a quiet place. We'd like to keep it that way. In the future, we'd appreciate it if you'd keep your workers under control."

The cop starts to walk away but my dad has to respond.

"I'm not a goddamn slave owner. My workers are free to come and go as they please."

The cop turns back. "Sir, if your workers are here illegally, that makes them criminals already."

I run downstairs and get out the first-aid kit. The policeman gets back in his car and drives off in a huff. By this time Steve is up too and everyone converges in the kitchen. My dad helps Tomás to a kitchen chair and has a good look at his injuries. Steve talks to Miguel, trying to understand what happened.

"Roar, get me a wet cloth."

I run the water till it's hot and get a washcloth out of

the hall closet. I soak it and hand it to my dad, who dabs Tomás's cheek. Tomás winces. My dad carefully cleans the wound and opens the first-aid kit. He disinfects the cut and tapes a dressing onto it. He takes a kitchen towel and fills it with ice cubes and presses it onto Tomás's eye. Tomás holds it there with his hand. Rufus licks Tomás's free hand. My dad pulls up Tomás's T-shirt. Ugly purple bruises are starting to appear along his rib cage. He touches them carefully, looking for fractures.

Steve is still talking to Miguel in Spanish and I can understand enough words and hand gestures to figure out what happened. This was no bar fight. This was a message for my dad sent by the other farmworkers, probably the same people who risked their lives alongside Tomás crossing the border into the U.S. and probably the same people who were at his side when Sylvia died. The message is "stop."

16

The heat continues on, as relentless as my dad and his lawsuit. The day after Tomás is beaten, we get calls from the local paper in Stockton, the *Sacramento Bee*, and even a left-wing Spanish newspaper that's printed in the Mission in San Francisco. Somehow my dad has become the unofficial spokesperson for a movement that the farmworkers are reluctant to own. He's a shepherd without a flock, a preacher without a congregation.

Our own little town is buzzing as people weigh in on the issue left and right. One thing I've noticed about the people around here is that everyone has an opinion. Small groups gather anywhere it's air-conditioned on Main Street to discuss the biggest thing that's happened around here since Skeeter "Dumb-ass" drove his pickup into the front window of the post office (the joke around town was that he thought it was a drive-through). Some people are speculating that the insurance company will settle quickly before this becomes the social justice event of the century and they end up looking like the bad guys. Other people are saying that it'll be a cool day in hell before an illegal wins a lawsuit against a citizen. The bad guy in this story keeps changing, depending on who you ask.

Tomás is fragile. He moves around the farm gingerly. His half-closed eye makes him look unbearably sad and I wish I could hug him and kick my dad in the knee at the same time. It's been decided that when Tomás is feeling better, he'll leave the farm and go to Reynaldo's vineyards to work there for a while until things in this county blow over. My dad is obviously willing to endure a lot of "I told you so" from Reynaldo to keep Tomás safe. Steve is on the fence, but he says that things have come too far to turn back. Miguel is quiet.

That afternoon, shortly after lunch, a gray haze settles over the sky. The sun shines vaguely through the cloud cover. I don't give it much thought—we never get rain like this—but as I'm gathering up bunches of washed radishes and tying them with twist ties, I feel a big fat drop on my scalp and then several more plop onto my bare arms and my face. I look up at the sky as the rain turns from drops to sheets and becomes a full-on shower, soaking through my Indian cotton dress and turning the dusty yard to mud. Rufus looks up too, confused. Rain like this can only be thought of in biblical terms. Locusts and a drought can't be far behind. I look around at Steve, Miguel, my dad, Tomás, scattered about the farm. They're all standing there, looking up. My dad has his arms spread wide. I know him; he'll consider this a sign. I dash into the house and grab my camera. This is not something I want to forget.

It rains like that for hours, washing everything clean. No one takes shelter. We must look like a farm family in a Kansas dust bowl at the end of a drought season. After days and days of unbearable heat, the rain is such a joyful and unexpected thing that everyone wants to experience it firsthand. I inhale the rich wet-earth scent, hoping to benefit from this miracle somehow. Coffee-colored puddles gather in the tractor tire ruts, and the chickens make a ruckus like they think the sky is falling.

I wish that Forest were here with me. I know that he would feel the same way about the rain as I do. I know that he would see the joy in it. He'd probably laugh as the rain splashed off his upturned face.

In the early evening, the clouds move off in giant, tumbling cotton balls and the blue sky reappears. The air is thick with humidity. It's Steve's turn to cook and he makes vegetarian lasagna with our summer squash and tomatoes and eggplant. While Steve cooks, Miguel and my dad load up the truck for tomorrow's market and restaurant deliveries. Tomás can't lift anything right now but he still insists on working.

We gather around the dinner table, our strange little family. This is Tomás's last dinner with us for a while but none of us seems to want to mention it. We speak quietly in Spanish and English, passing salad, bread, wine, and water. Ali Farka Toure plays African blues on the stereo in the living room. Rufus lies on Tomás's feet as though he knows what's coming and doesn't like it at all. He still smells like wet dog.

After dinner I do the dishes, and the kitchen empties out. My dad has a meeting with his sustainable farming group and Steve goes to meet a friend for a guitar jam session. Miguel and Tomás go to the bunkhouse. As soon as I see my dad's taillights on the driveway I dial Forest's cell phone. He picks up on the first ring.

"Hi."

"Did you see the rain?" I ask.

"I saw it. I was at the library and I had to get out there and walk in it."

"I knew you would."

"It was crazy, wasn't it?"

"It was beautiful. I got soaked."

"Me too. How come you can call?"

"My dad's at a meeting."

"For how long?"

"A couple of hours, tops."

"Can you come out?"

"Maybe. For a little while."

"Can I come over there? I want to say good-bye to Tomás."

"He's coming back, you know."

"I know."

"Okay. Come right now."

Forest arrives twelve minutes later. I send him out to the bunkhouse on his own. He's been practicing his Spanish for occasions like this.

I watch from the porch swing. He knocks on the bunkhouse door and Miguel opens it. They shake hands and Forest stands there with his hands on his hips, looking awkward. Tomás appears and they do that thing that people do when they don't speak the same language. They each say a few words and nod a lot. Forest surprises Tomás by hugging him. Tomás hesitates. Mexican men don't hug each other much. He halfheartedly hugs back.

Forest and I chase each other through the tall, fragrant grass to the cathedral of trees. Inside it feels cool. The sun has already disappeared behind the trees. We sit on the damp ground in our spot in the middle, cross-legged, facing each other, and catch our breath. The damp is seeping through our clothes. He takes my hands in his and I watch his face change to shadows as dusk approaches. In a few moments, when darkness closes in on us, I lean forward and kiss him. His tongue touches my lips and my front teeth. I touch his tongue with mine and taste licorice. He pulls me onto his lap and I drape my arm around his narrow shoulders. He kisses me deeper and longer than he ever has before. I close my eyes and let it happen. When I open my eyes, I watch his white fingers trace the side of my sun-browned thigh up to my hip bone and farther. I marvel at the contrast of our skin colors and a delicious chill runs up my spine. I lose myself in Forest and give up all control over what happens next until I remember where we are. I grab Forest's wrist from under my T-shirt and look at his watch.

"Oh my God! It's late. We have to get back."

"Five more minutes," he whispers.

"No. We have to go. Your car's in the driveway."

"Three minutes . . . please."

I untangle myself and get up, pulling Forest to his feet. I wish we could stay here all night together. Maybe I could brave this place on the graveyard shift, maybe not. I'm already hearing some strange rustlings in the trees. Besides, if the vampires don't kill us my dad surely will. Plus, I have to admit that I'm a little bit afraid of where this thing with Forest is heading. I've envisioned it and dreamed it and longed for it. Most importantly, I've wanted it to happen with Forest. There's no question about that, but it's like there's an invisible line I can't quite cross over until I feel like it's really right. Sometimes I wish my mom were around to talk to about these things. She was always very frank and open about sex. We never had cute little names for parts of the body. A vagina was a vagina and a penis was a penis. When I was seven I asked her where babies come from. She sat me right down and told me everything in graphic detail as though I'd asked her to explain how a combustion engine works. I was more prepared for my period than any girl in my grade but I was the last to get it, and when it finally arrived my mom wasn't around anymore.

Forest and I have a hard time finding the path through the tall grass in the darkness until our eyes adjust. The cool grass whips at our skin as we dash toward the lights of the farm like scared children, all thoughts of romance cast aside for now. Forest kisses me good-bye next to his car and takes off down the road. My dad's pickup turns into the drive moments later.

The next morning my dad drives into the city for the market. He'll stop in Berkeley to pick up Jane on the way. She's going to work the market in Steve's place. Steve and I will take Tomás the next county over to Reynaldo's place. None of us is making a big deal about it because we all want to believe that it's temporary. I sit in the back of Steve's lumbering Jeep with Tomás's small duffel next to me on the seat. Tomás is quiet in the passenger seat as we cross over from farm country to wine country. The red grapes are dusky and heavy on the vine and the green grapes look plump and ripe. The grapes in this valley are too valuable to be machine-picked. They're all picked by humans, which is why it's so important that the vineyard workers keep coming back every year. They keep this business alive. There's a lot of money to be made picking grapes too. The vineyard workers make more than farmworkers. In a two-month grape harvest, on the right crew, grape pickers can clear up to seven thousand dollars. That's enough to buy a small piece of land in Mexico, and maybe some chickens and a few goats. People who visit the Napa Valley never see these workers. They're invisible.

We turn off the main highway and travel down a dirt road to one of Reynaldo's vineyards. As we pull into the yard we see Reynaldo at the controls of a tractor as it lifts a giant plastic container filled with grapes and dumps it into the bed of a huge truck. He's wearing a striped shirt with the sleeves rolled up and a trucker's cap. He waves when he sees us and shuts down the tractor. Tomás gets out of the Jeep slowly and we walk over to Reynaldo. The yard is busy with forklifts and workers coming and going. The smell is familiar to me: fermented grapes and oak. Reynaldo kisses my cheek and hugs me with his beefy brown arms and then he shakes hands with Steve and Tomás, speaking Spanish in a serious tone. I can see Tomás relaxing. Reynaldo has a way of putting people at ease. I'm happy that Tomás will at least be here with Reynaldo, where we can check in on him. Whatever Reynaldo thinks of the situation, he'll put it aside and do the right thing for someone who came from the same place and probably the same conditions as he did.

Steve and I say our good-byes to Tomás, who looks to me like a child being abandoned on the first day of school by his mother. We get back into the Jeep and Reynaldo puts a case of wine in the back. We head back to the main road and stop for cold drinks at an overpriced little boutique grocery store meant for tourists. While Steve gets the drinks, I wander over to the newspaper stand. The headline of the *Wine Country Observer* catches my eye:

DIABLO COUNTY MIGRANT FARMWORKER SUES DEVELOPMENT RESIDENT FOR WRONGFUL DEATH

Steve comes out the door of the grocery with a soda in each hand. I show him the paper. He sighs.

"Reynaldo already knows about that. He's giving Tomás a new name while he's here and a good backstory. Don't worry, he'll be okay. No one's expecting him to be out here."

I must not look convinced because Steve lifts up my ponytail and puts the cold soda against the back of my neck.

"Hey!"

"That's the spirit. Now get in the Jeep. You're driving home."

"What?"

"You heard me."

Steve's Jeep isn't exactly a high-performance vehicle. I push in the clutch with my left foot and wiggle the gearshift around, looking for reverse. I move my right foot from the brake to the gas and press down. The Jeep shoots forward and a couple of tourists run for their lives.

"Little farther left. Try again," says Steve, not the slightest bit alarmed.

I yank the gearshift over and toward me and try the gas again. This time we move backward. I ease out of our parking spot and then start over, looking for first gear now. I find it and we move toward the exit. I'm sweating profusely.

"Good job," says Steve, popping almonds into his mouth.

I ease onto the road, looking both ways first. The Jeep sounds like a Sherman tank in first so I push in the clutch and find second gear. Now we're lurching along at about twenty miles an hour. Cars are passing me impatiently.

"Pick up the pace, Grandma, we'll be late for church."

"Shut up."

I find third easily and speed up to about forty-five miles an hour. I start to relax. I look over at Steve and grin.

"How am I doing?"

"Fantastic."

"I'm driving in wine country!"

"Yup. Okay, now pass this loser. Check your mirror, shoulder check, and then the mirror again. One, two, three, and then signal and make your move."

I do it just like he says and I pass my first car ever. I'm drunk with power. Steve starts digging around on the floor.

"Steve?" I need him up here with me.

"Relax, you're cool." He waves a CD. "Got it, *Taj Mahal*." He slides it into the player. Good driving music, very relaxing. I look around at the passing vineyards. The view from the driver's side is entirely different. You see the world through your own hands on the wheel. I love the way driving makes me feel. It's like you're in control but you're also a little *out* of control.

Steve puts his feet up on the dash and taps his foot to the music. "Okay, Roar, remember road rule number one?"

"Yes."

"Well?"

"Drive defensively, and by defensively I mean assume everyone else on the road is an idiot."

"Good girl."

The wind pulls at my hair as I steer the Jeep down the road toward home.

17

"His name's Marty and he works at Blockbuster," says Storm, describing her latest boyfriend.

"Do you get free video rentals?"

"Yeah." She sighs. "Plus all the Milk Duds I can eat." She stirs her coffee slowly.

"So, why so glum, chum?"

"I sort of miss Doo-wayne."

"Doo-wayne lives in a trailer park in Stockton with his girlfriend and their baby. Do you really want that for yourself?"

"No, of course not. He had a lot of energy, though; I liked that."

"What about Marty? Marty sounds nice."

"Marty just got out of rehab and he's a little . . . fragile."

"Like how?"

"Well, like he's sort of sad all the time and there's a whole long list of things I'm not allowed to talk about and places we're not allowed to go, including bars, of course."

"Storm, you're sixteen. You're not supposed to be in bars anyway."

"I like bars. I like the fancy drinks. Yesterday Marty and I went for Slurpees."

"Flavor?"

"Cream soda. Then we started making out in the back of his sad Volvo and he started crying."

"Has it ever occurred to you that you don't have to date anyone for a while, that you could take a break from guys?"

"No."

"Well, it might actually do you some good. You could read a book or get a hobby."

"I *have* a hobby. It's men. And who am I supposed to hang out with during this 'break'"—she uses finger quotes—"you and Forest? That would be great. I could watch the two of you almost have sex over and over again. How fun for me."

"Okay, never mind. Have your parents met Marty?"

"Yes. He told them all about rehab. That's another thing. He tells *everyone* about rehab. It's some sort of bizarre coming-clean crap that they teach you on the inside. Do you think that the guy at the mini-mart cares that you just got out of rehab?"

"So, did your parents like him?"

Storm rolls her eyes. "My mom asked him if she could include him in her prayers."

"What'd he say?"

"Yes. And that's revolting."

Millie's not working today but a sweet-looking girl with limp blond hair, who I recognize from our school, takes our order. She seems afraid of Storm. Storm has a not-so-subtle way of letting you know how she feels about you. It's been known to wither even the toughest of girls.

"I'll have a burger, and could you tell Juan that it's for me? He grills it just the way I like it." She barely looks at the girl.

The girl nods, scribbling on her pad furiously.

I'm extra friendly to try to make up for Storm. "I'll have a grilled cheese with sliced tomatoes." I smile at her reassuringly. "That's a cute watch." I point to her Hello Kitty wristwatch.

"Thanks." The girl blushes and disappears with our unopened menus.

Storm looks at me, bemused. "'Cute watch?' What, are you running for mayor?"

I ignore her.

"So, how are things on the farm? You people have the whole town talking, I'm sure you know that." She picks up a knife and uses it as a mirror to examine her lips.

"Yes, of course I know that."

She puts down the knife. "Man, your dad's really kicked up some crap around here. Did you know that they're calling him a communist?"

"That's ridiculous. Who's calling him that?"

She points out the window, indicating everyone in town. "Them, but they're idiots. I told them your dad's a socialist. Anyone can see that."

"You're telling people that? What makes you think he's a socialist?"

She holds up a fist. "You know, power to the people, and all that crap."

"I think you mean activist."

"Whatever. By the way, Brody Burk has officially blown a gasket over all this. He organized a meeting."

"A meeting? With who?"

"I dunno, Klansmen probably."

"You're joking, right?"

She shrugs.

"What was the meeting about?"

"I forget what he called it, something about patriotism and the American way and all that bullshit. Don't worry about it, I'm sure it was just a bunch of good old boys, drinking too much and blowing off steam."

I don't even want to think about what Brody does to "blow off steam."

"Oh, okay, and if I wake up to a burning cross on my lawn, I'll know who to point a finger at."

"Well, if I were you I would just put it out with a garden hose. Pointing a finger at Brody never did anyone around here much good." She looks suddenly bored and moves on. "Hey, did I tell you about the Manolo Blahniks I scored on eBay?"

"No."

"Oh my GOD! They're gorgeous: Kelly green leather Mary Janes with three-inch stacked heels."

"They sound fabulous."

"And they are." She looks out the diner window. "Hey, isn't that your dad?"

It *is* my dad. I'm about to knock on the glass when I realize that he's not alone. He's walking next to a woman. It takes me a minute to figure out that the woman is Forest's mom.

"Isn't that Connie Gilwood?" asks Storm. "Wow, what happened to *her*?"

It seems that something did happen to her. Her hair is pulled back into a thin ponytail, revealing an unmade-up face and glasses. *Glasses?* She's wearing jeans and a plain white T-shirt and her torpedo boobs seem to have lost their oomph. She's about half the size I remember her being at the farmers' market that day. Forest never mentioned that his mom had changed so much physically. There's a delicate sadness in her face that I never noticed before. Maybe it wasn't even there before.

"What do you suppose she's doing with my dad?"

As they head up the street, Storm cranes her neck to watch. "Um, hugging him."

We watch in disbelief. I grab my camera off the seat and snap a photo of it. They don't hug like they're in love but it's like they know each other pretty well. Connie gets into a car and pulls away from the curb, and my dad gives her a little wave and walks the other way. I'm stunned.

Storm turns back around in her seat. "Well, that was interesting. Looks like you can tell your dad about Forest now. Hey, maybe the four of you could double-date!"

I glare at her.

After I choke down my grilled cheese and try unsuccessfully to rush Storm through her burger, she drops me off at the end of the driveway and I walk up the road to the house. My dad's truck is gone. Miguel and Steve are working far enough out that all I have to do is wave, which is lucky because I'd hate for them to see the look on my face. I stomp up the stairs to my dad's room and start pulling open drawers and digging through his stuff. I have no idea what I'm looking for or if I'm even looking for anything. I might just be vandalizing the place. After I've rifled through all his dresser drawers I yank open his closet door. There's a shoebox on the top shelf that I have to stand on my tiptoes to reach. I still can't quite get it so I jump up and wiggle it forward a bit at a time. Suddenly the whole box comes down on my head, spilling its contents onto the floor around me. The first thing I grab off the floor is a photo. It's my mom and some guy with a beard. They're standing barefoot on a sandy beach in front of a palm tree, smiling. They look tan and happy. My mom looks like her old self. She's wearing a white cotton sundress and she's holding a plump little baby girl with wavy black hair and blue eyes who looks a lot like me, but it's not me. I turn it over. My mom's handwriting says: *Me and Buddy with our daughter, Deirdre, Key West, Christmas*. She didn't write the year; is that because she knows that my dad would know it and add it to the other Christmas photos from other years? I sink to the floor, staring at the photo of my mom in her shiny new life with her new boyfriend and her new daughter. Well, what was I thinking would happen? Did I think she'd just arrive home and start being my mom again? What a stupid, stupid girl I've been.

I dig through the papers on the floor around me. I find

several opened letters addressed to my dad with a return address in Key West, Florida. I arrange them in order of the dates on the postmarks and pull open the first one. In my mom's handwriting, she asks how he's doing and she says that she found him through our old neighbors in San Francisco. She tells him that she's clean and sober and she's started a new life in Florida. She asks about me and she includes a phone number where she can be reached.

In the second letter she gets right to the point. She says that she wants to remarry and she asks why my dad won't sign the divorce papers that her lawyers in Florida sent. I dig around and find a big envelope with a Florida law firm on the return address. The postmark is dated a year ago.

The letters from my mom start to sound a little insistent. She wants to know why he won't let her get on with her life. She doesn't mention me in any of these letters. Why would she? She wants to move on. She's started a new life. Why would she want me around to remind her of the mess she made of her old one? There are a few smaller envelopes from her Florida lawyers referring to my dad's "cavalier" attitude and urging him to take this matter seriously.

Among the business-size envelopes, there's a square unopened envelope addressed to me. I tear it open. It's a birthday card with a painting of a bouquet of flowers on the front. The kind that you buy in big boxes so you're ready for any occasion, the kind of card you send to someone who lives in a nursing home. Inside it says:

Warmest Wishes for a Happy Birthday!

It's signed: *Love, Mom*

I grab all the letters off the floor and stuff them back into the box. I replace the lid and carry the box downstairs. I dial Forest's cell. When he picks up I collapse in tears.

Forest picks me up at the house a few minutes later. There's no point in keeping things between us a secret anymore. My dad's the king of secrets. We drive to the tar pits and I dump the box of letters out onto the seat of Forest's car. I show him everything. My cheeks are streaked with tears. He pulls me across the seat to him and I cry on his shoulder, not caring that his T-shirt is getting soaked in tears and snot, not caring that I'm squashing all the letters. He doesn't say a word. He just holds me like that for a long time, running his hand over my hair, while I sob.

After a while I just can't cry anymore. I stop and look up at Forest.

"And did you know that I saw my dad with your mom today? Did you even know that they knew each other?"

"No. I mean, I heard her on the phone once and I knew she was talking to some man I didn't know. I sure didn't think it was your dad, though."

"Do you think they're . . . ? You know."

"No. I don't think so."

"What am I going to do?" I ask him.

"Well. Don't you think you should go talk to him?"

"Yeah. I guess. Can't we just run away? Please ask me right now and I'll go. I mean it. Ask me. If you love me you'll ask me."

He looks at me and I know that he's taking me seriously. "Okay, I'll ask you. I'll ask you after you talk to him."

I sigh. "Okay." He's right. If I left like that I'd be doing exactly what my mom did.

Forest drops me off after assuring me over and over again that I just have to call and he'll be right over. He wasn't too specific about what he would do once he got here but I think he'd do anything, including letting me cry on his sleeve some more.

My dad's truck is sitting in the driveway looking as guilty as an old truck can look.

I climb the porch stairs indignantly and yank the screen door open. The incriminating shoebox is tucked firmly under my arm. My dad is on the phone in the kitchen.

"I need to talk to you."

He signals at me to wait and then he sees the box. "Ned, I'll call you back," he says. He hangs up the phone.

"Honey. I was going to talk to you about that."

"Don't 'honey' me! You know that you weren't."

"Yes, I was. I just wanted you to get to a place where you could understand it a little better."

"I understand, all right. In case you hadn't noticed. I lost my MOM! You could have at least confirmed that for me, let me know that NO, she isn't coming back . . . EVER! Instead of moving me to this godforsaken place and forcing me to be a stupid farmer and keeping me in the dark about everything! None of this stupid life we live was my idea. Have you ever considered that? Have you ever once even asked me if I'm happy? The answer to that is NO. You have not. You just run around like some new-age hippie revolutionary, trying to save the world! Well, I'm your daughter! How come you never tried to save me?"

My dad sits there and watches as I break down into sobs again. Then he stands up and lurches for me, partly to hug me and partly to keep me from falling. We stay like that for a while.

"You're right. I'm sorry. I'm so sorry. I'm so sorry." He whispers it into my ear and holds on to me. This is only the second time he's hugged me since we moved out here and the other time was only a few days ago. He says sorry a thousand times. Then he slowly lets go of me and looks into my swollen eyes.

"I've been a jerk. I got so caught up in my own loneliness that I forgot about yours."

"Did you divorce her?" I ask, wiping my nose on my forearm.

"Yes. She wanted it. I couldn't put her off anymore."

"Do you still love her?"

He looks away.

"Yes." His eyes fill with tears. "I'm okay, though. I really am." He wipes his eyes.

"I know."

"Your mom . . ." He starts and then falters. "Your mom was wonderful, you know that, but, well, she has problems. She has a habit of making a mess of things and then moving on without considering the people she's left behind. Maybe she has things sorted out now, maybe not."

I think about that baby girl in the photo who looks like me. Will she end up, years from now, in the same place I am right now?

"Roar, I don't think she meant to hurt us. It's all part of her sickness, the depression, the drinking, everything. It's something she couldn't control. I hope you can forgive her someday."

"We'll see." I stick out my chin defiantly.

"You know, it was even harder for me when you started looking just like her."

"I can't help it."

"I know. You're as beautiful as she was the day I met her."

I ignore that. I don't want to look like her. I'm nothing like her.

"Speaking of meeting people. What were you doing with Connie Gilwood today?"

He looks like I just punched him in the stomach. He inhales and sits down again.

"A couple of weeks ago, Connie called me. She wanted to see me. She wanted me to understand her side of what happened that day. She said that if she didn't tell someone she would go crazy."

"And do you understand?"

"I don't know. I know that the woman we saw that day isn't who she is. I think she was in a lot of pain. She still is. She's getting better, though."

"Aren't you supposed to be archenemies? I thought you hated development people."

"No. I guess I just hate developments."

"So you're friends?"

"I suppose we are, in a strange way. I've seen her a couple of times and I've talked to her on the phone. She wants to meet Tomás and tell him how sorry she is."

"What did you tell her?"

"I said we should wait until Tomás has had a bit of time to heal."

"Why didn't you tell me?"

"I don't know. I didn't think I could expect you to understand."

"How is this whole lawsuit thing going to work without a villain?"

"Don't worry, there's plenty of villains left in this lawsuit. We're dealing with an insurance company . . . and lawyers, remember?"

"Dad, I have to tell you something."

I sit down at the table and my dad pours me a glass of water. I'm dehydrated from crying gallons of tears. I tell him all about Forest. I watch his face go from shock to anger to acceptance. He calmly proposes that we stop sneaking around behind each other's backs like we're in some sort of weird television drama. He tells me that he wants to meet him, this boy I've told him so much about.

18

I punch the numbers carefully into the phone. I try not to hear my heart thudding all the way into my temples. I sit there flicking toast crumbs across the kitchen table as the phone lines do their thing and the other end starts ringing. My heart thuds louder in my head. A man picks up. His voice is gruff, a bit salty-doggish. Buddy, I presume. Maybe he's a pirate. No, there are no pirates named Buddy.

"Hello?"

"Hi. Is Gabriella there?" This is the first time I've ever called my mother by her name. I realize that I'm not really prepared for her to be there. For some reason I thought that this would be a message-on-voice-mail thing and then the ball would be in her court.

"Hang on, I'll get her," says Buddy. I hear his footsteps and then his voice calling her and then my mother's voice in the background just as I remember it and also the voice of a small child. I close my eyes and picture palm trees and sand. Sometimes when one day started to look like another out here on the farm, I imagined that there was another me living with my mom all this time. I imagined us going to galleries and thrift stores and having adventures together. I never pictured us in Florida. I always pictured us at our old house in the city.

After a few seconds my mom comes on the line just like she's always been waiting there, ten digits away.

"Hello?" Her voice is a bit tentative, the way it is when you have a past.

"Hi. It's Roar." My heart picks up speed.

Silence. I wasn't expecting silence but there it is. Dead air.

"Roar, honey! Hi! It's so good to hear your voice. What a nice surprise!"

I want to believe that this is the way a mother talks to a daughter she hasn't seen in two years but it sounds so much more like the way you would talk to someone who was in your high school graduating class, who's just passing through town and wants to catch up.

"So, how are you doing?" she asks.

"Um, I'm good. How about you?"

"Well, we're good. Great, actually."

She said "*we're* good" as in a *unit*, a *family*.

"So, what's Florida like?" I ask.

"Oh, it's beautiful here, just beautiful. Buddy has a sport fishing boat that he takes the tourists out on. It's a good little business and I do the books and chase after our little girl, Deirdre. She just started walking the other day."

But I'm your little girl, remember?

"Well, that sounds great," I say, as phony as can be.

"It is. It's so great. Well, except for the odd hurricane, but every place has its hazards, isn't that right? San Francisco had earthquakes."

And us. San Francisco had us.

"Did your dad tell you to call?" she asks.

"No, he doesn't know I'm calling."

"Is he doing all right?"

"He's fine. We're farmers now." That came out weird, like I'm announcing that we're Quakers or something. Somehow, the deeper I get into this conversation, the less I want to tell her.

"I just can't imagine your dad farming."

That's funny, I can't imagine you as the wife of a fisherman named Buddy.

"Well, he's actually pretty good at it," I say, perhaps a hair more defensively than necessary. She seems not to have heard me, though.

"Hang on a second. I want you to say hi to someone."

"Um, okay."

"Sweetie?" calls my mom, and I start to answer her until I realize that she isn't talking to me.

"Come here, sweetie," she coaxes. "Say hi to your big sister."

"No!" says a little voice.

"Come on, sweetie. Say HI!"

"HI!" says the little voice.

God, why do people do that?

"Hi." I feel like an idiot.

"Say bye-bye!" says my mom.

"BYE-BYE!" yells the little voice.

"Bye." But she's already gone. I can hear her yelling in the background.

My mom comes back on the phone. "You two really should meet. Wouldn't that be great?"

"Yeah, great."

"You know, I should really get going. This monster's got to go down for a nap or there'll be hell to pay later."

"Yeah, okay, me too. I have to go."

"Wow. It's sure been nice talking to you. I'm *so* glad you called. You just call me anytime you like, okay?"

"Okay, sure," I say, knowing that I'll never call again.

"Oh, and Roar?"

"Yeah?"

"Have a wonderful birthday."

"Thanks."

"Bye, now."

"Bye." I click the phone off and sit in my chair, feeling numb and wondering what just happened. I think back to before I dialed the phone and try to recall what I was expecting to happen. Was I thinking that my mom would beg me to come live with her and her new family in Florida? I guess not, but maybe I wanted to believe that she'd been waiting a long time for that call and my dad was the only thing preventing it and now that we were back in touch, she could resume her role as my mother somehow. Not only is she not interested in that job, I think she would have been happier if the call had never happened at all and she'd never had to deal with the dregs of her old life.

I feel another wave of tears coming on, but even though my bottom lip starts to quiver and I feel pinpricks behind my eyes, the tears never arrive. I guess I must be all cried out.

I dial Forest's cell and, because he's on twenty-four-hour alert, he picks up immediately.

"Hi," I say quietly.

"So, how did it go?" he asks.

"Um, well, I think I got what they call 'closure.'"

"Oh, Roar. I'm sorry."

"Well. It appears that she's moved on and so should I. I suppose it's just as well. It would have been nice just to hear her say 'I've missed you,' though."

"I'm sure she's missed you, but if she says it she has to acknowledge all the guilt she's felt for the past two years and she probably doesn't want to go there. It's messy."

"You're probably right." I sigh.

"Hey, let's do something. I'll come get you, okay?"

"No, I'm all icky. I think I want to be alone."

"Okay."

In a movie of the week, this would be the part of the story where the lead character:

A) Runs away to the nearest dangerous city, where trouble lurks around every corner.

B) Goes off and gets drunk and then smashes up a car.

C) Has unprotected sex with her boyfriend and gets pregnant.

D) Steals something and gets caught.

E) Any combination of the above.

As if on cue, my phone rings. I half expect it to be my mom, feeling bad about the phone call, wanting to apologize. She was distracted, but now the baby is napping and she has time to really talk.

It's not my mom; it's Storm, psychically responding

to a need for rebellion.

"What are you doing?" she demands.

"Contemplating something drastic," I respond.

"Oh, pish posh, I'm picking you up in ten minutes. I stole my mom's car, or rather, borrowed it."

"Where are we going?"

"Oakdale county fair. If we hurry we can catch the hog-calling competition."

Storm, as promised, arrives in ten minutes, driving a late-model Buick with a large crucifix dangling from the rearview mirror and a "Jesus Saves" bumper sticker on the back.

I get in the car wearing dark wraparound sunglasses to hide my puffy eyes.

"Hey, homey," says Storm, taking in my sunglasses. She's dressed in an outfit that the fairgoers won't soon forget. A red-and-white-checkered halter top and denim cutoff short shorts with a belt that features a huge rodeo buckle—a gift from Doo-wayne, I gather, although he probably doesn't know he "gave" it to her. She has a long cigarette between her fingers and she's wearing oversized Jackie O sunglasses.

"Hey, I have a gift for you." I hand her the white leather go-go boots. She pushes her sunglasses onto the top of her head and tosses the cigarette out the window. Storm is the archenemy of Smoky the Bear.

"Are you kidding me? Those are for me?"

"Yup."

She pulls off her four-inch platform sandals, throws them into the backseat, and yanks the boots on. The look in her eyes is pure lust. I've never seen anyone fall in love with footwear like that.

"These are freaking fabulous!" she says, admiring her feet. "How have I lived so long without these babies?"

"You mean you're going to wear them? It's eighty degrees out."

She puts the car in gear and hits the gas. "And your point would be . . . ?"

There are a thousand things you can do at a county fair and Storm intends to do most of them. The first order of business is food. We load up on cotton candy, caramel apples, and Tom Thumb donuts. Then we go on the Ferris wheel, the Tilt-A-Whirl, the Matterhorn, the swings that go around until you vomit (in a unique role reversal, Storm holds *my* hair out of my face), and the haunted house. Then we start over with corn on the cob, greasy onion rings, and saltwater taffy. After that we climb the metal stands at the competition ring (not easy in white go-go boots) and find a good seat to watch the hog-calling competition. The air is scented with sawdust and animal poop and the stands are filled with cowboys and 4-H parents. After the hog-calling competition (which is truly surreal), the program continues with cowboys riding ostriches and endless 4-H club competitions where children dressed like miniature cowboys and cowgirls parade their pig/cow/sheep/goat/horse around the ring while a judge dressed in a peacock blue western-style polyester leisure suit stands in the middle and decides which animal wins a ribbon, which apparently has nothing to do with how cute the kid is. As the winner is announced, crying ensues among the losing cowboys and cowgirls. That part was hard to watch. I take a ton of photos of the world of heartbreak that is 4-H competition. Storm flirts shamelessly with any man within flirting distance and adds vodka to her lemonade from a discreet silver flask she carries in her purse.

We wander back to the midway as it's getting dark and the colored lights come on everywhere, lighting up the rides and the booths like tie-dye Christmas. The effect is a slice of small-town America that you don't see much anymore. The air is filled with laughter and screaming and carnival music. We play the ring toss and the dart game, which I'm especially good at. I can also squirt water into a clown's mouth like nobody's business and I win a stuffed monkey with Velcro on its paws that Storm wears around her neck like a mink stole for the rest of the night. As

Storm's chatting up the guy who runs the funhouse, I spy a pay phone and dig out some change and call Forest.

"Hey, are you okay? Why do I hear calliope music?"

"Um, I'm at the county fair in Oakdale."

"Why?"

"I don't really know."

"Who are you with?"

"Storm." I glance over at her; she's leaning over as the funhouse guy lights her cigarette. Even from here, I can see her batting her eyelashes.

"Is she drinking?"

"Is that a rhetorical question?"

"Don't let her drive."

"Right, you're right. I won't."

"Call me when you get home, okay?"

"I will."

He's about to hang up when I suddenly feel brave. "Hey, Forest."

"Yeah?"

"I love you."

"Really?"

"Yeah."

"You're not saying that because you think you might die tonight, are you?"

"No."

"Good. Call me later."

"Bye."

I head back over to Storm, who's now writing her phone number on a matchbook cover for funhouse guy. I coax her away from his wolflike grin and we find the saltwater taffy place again so I can bring a bag home for Forest. He surely deserves it for absorbing all my salty tears on his shirt.

We make our way back to the parking lot and lie across the windshield of Storm's mom's car and watch the fireworks that they shoot off every night when the fairground closes. Even though I've never driven at night, I trust myself more than I do Storm so I wrestle the keys away from her and carefully guide the car through the grassy parking lot, driving like an old woman until I see the sign for the freeway. Storm sings along to a hip-hop song on the radio and then falls asleep, making her the worst copilot ever. I figure I'll just drive super slow and we should be okay. At least there aren't gears to wrestle with. This car practically drives itself. I look out the windshield into the darkness and the heaviness starts creeping back into my heart. I push it away, promising myself that I'll deal with it later. Fortunately, driving takes all of my focus. I drive to Storm's house and put the car keys on the seat so no one thinks that Storm drove in her condition. I leave her snoring in the passenger seat and steal her brand-new, hardly ever used bike out of the dark garage and pedal the five miles home. I'm really grateful that there's air in the tires. It's exhilarating riding alone down the empty road in the dark.

Later, I'm lying in bed. Rufus is curled up next to me on the floor. I watch the curtains ripple in the breeze, which has returned with the cooler air. I remember reading somewhere that humans have tribal tendencies, and as we go through life we're inclined to gather people who are like us and form bonds with them that can be stronger than familial bonds. This thing with my mom is just a wound that has to heal. If I dwell on it, it will infect and fester and the healing will take a lot longer. If I leave it alone, the pain will lessen every day and one day it will disappear completely like when you finally flick a scab off and there's new pink skin underneath. In the meantime, I have my own little tribe. I have people in my life who care about me, and it doesn't really matter where or who I came from. The only thing that matters is where I'm going.

I pick up the phone to dial Forest but when I click it on, my dad's on it. I eavesdrop for a few seconds. He's speaking Spanish and then I hear Tomás's voice responding.

"Tomás?" I ask.

"Sí. ¿Aurora?"

"Yes."

"¿Que hubo?" Which means *what's up?*

"Not much," I answer.

"Dad, when's he coming back?" I ask.

"I don't know. Soon, I hope."

"Can you tell him that I miss him?"

He tells Tomás in Spanish and Tomás responds.

"He says he misses you too and he hopes to come back soon," says my dad.

"Adios, Tomás."

"*Nos vemos*, Aurora," says Tomás, which means *see you later*.

I click the phone off. I wait a few minutes until I can't hear my dad's voice downstairs anymore, then I call Forest and whisper good night.

19

*T*he morning after the county fair I wake up late and rush out the door to take care of the loathsome chickens so that I can get into the darkroom and develop the photos from the fair. I have a good feeling about some of them and I can't wait to get to work. I take the bowl of table scraps next to the sink out with me. The chickens eat vegetable scraps and what they don't eat we put on the compost heap. Today they get potato peels, carrot peels, radish tops, and leftover brown rice. The chickens are noisier than usual as I pass the coop on the way to the supply shed to get the rest of their feed. Bruce, the rooster, who usually stays near the chickens, is over by the bunkhouse, pacing back and forth nervously like Mick Jagger. I fill up the metal feed bucket and head back to the coop. On my way, I notice a few chicken feathers clinging to the grass. A little farther along I see a couple of drops of dark red blood and then a few more. By the time I get to the coop, the events of the previous night become pretty obvious. There's a tiny hole dug under the chicken wire. It's much too small for an animal to have squeezed under the fence, but foxes are cunning and he probably just stuck his paw under the fence and grabbed the first chicken that walked by. The scene is grisly, feathers and blood everywhere, but no sign of the poor chicken. The remaining chickens, and I count them, are fine but extremely agitated. It's Gretta, I realize. The coyote got Gretta. I open the little wooden door and crawl into the coop and fill the feeders, but no one makes a move to leave the coop or to eat. I sit cross-legged on the floor of the coop in the dirt and try to make myself look like a chicken. I watch them do that frenetic worrying thing that chickens do. Perhaps I've grossly underestimated the sensitivity of the average chicken. They say that elephants mourn their dead. I think chickens might too. Apparently, watching one of their own get devoured alive has put them off their breakfast. Maybe they're fasting in support of their lost chicken sister. Maybe this is a wake. I went to a wake once when my dad's friend Ernie died. Everyone brought chicken. What does a chicken bring to a wake?

I know that soon I'll have to go get Steve or my dad and we'll have to take care of this hole and reinforce the area somehow, but something inspires me to sit there awhile among the fussing, clucking chickens and experience their loss with them.

As I sit on the dirt floor, I think about how, until yesterday, I unconsciously reserved a place on this farm for my mom even though I had no idea if she'd ever see it. I often pictured her taking part in the victories and the losses of our little operation, and whenever I did a chore or took on a project, I carried on a running dialogue, explaining in detail what I was doing, as I imagined my mother looking on with interest, eager to learn. Even the little things like planting a seedling properly or hanging out the laundry or removing the corn from a cob, I would share all of it with her. And now, twenty-four hours after our conversation, all that is in the past. I'm the "woman" of the farm now. I feel a sense of loss but I also feel oddly powerful. No matter what I do in my life, I'll always know that I can do almost any job on a farm that a man can do and I can probably do it just as well. I made my dad feel bad about dragging me out here but I was only trying to punish him. There's something about farmwork that makes you feel whole and strong. Maybe it's the closeness to the earth, maybe it's just being out here in all this open space, but now that I've lived this way I can't imagine not living this way.

A few minutes pass and the chickens slowly, tentatively

make their way over to the food. They watch me in that strange way that birds have of looking at you sideways. They're getting on with their chicken lives and I feel happy for them, as I do for myself. Moving on with your life is something you can learn from a chicken? Who knew?

I slowly get to my feet and go looking for someone to help me repair the coop.

Later in the afternoon, I'm clipping a print to my darkroom clothesline. It's a black-and-white eight-by-ten of a petite curly-haired little girl in purple chaps and a matching cowboy hat being nudged in the butt by a black-faced sheep. She's about four years old and the look on her face says that the sheep might be in big trouble. The phone over in the barn starts ringing and I hear my dad answer it. Then I hear a whoop. I'm not sure it's a whoop for joy. He's not a whooper by nature and strange things have been happening to my dad lately that have kept me vigilant; like today he went to pick up a couple of laborers at the post office to help with the clearing of a new field we're planning for root vegetables, and no one would get in the truck with him. This is unheard of. The day laborers will take any kind of work offered but they wouldn't even talk to my dad. Then someone flattened my dad's tires while he was parked in town the other night. He had to call Steve to come pick him up. He says it's just kids being kids, but I know he doesn't believe that. I fly out the door of the darkroom to find my dad, all in one piece, still on the phone, smiling. I stand there watching him and it occurs to me that I've been looking at him without seeing him for a long time. His long hair, falling in wisps from his trucker's cap, has some new gray streaks in it and I hadn't noticed the deep lines around his eyes and his mouth before. The hand holding the phone is calloused and weathered from farmwork. He talks for another minute and then hangs up the phone.

"What's going on?" I ask.

"The insurance company is settling."

"What does that mean, exactly?"

"It means that we won! I mean Tomás won. They're offering a fraction of what we asked for but Ned's got them on the run. He knows he can get more."

I swell with pride for him. He worked so hard for this. I remember all the times I doubted him. I feel bad about that. I'm pretty sure that he knew that all this could be for nothing but he still wouldn't quit. He just wanted what was right. My dad measures success in small victories.

"Can Tomás come home now?"

"Yes."

I hug him. He hugs back. This is our new thing, this thing where we hug. He goes off to tell Steve and Miguel.

I go back to my darkroom and clean up. I can't wait to tell Forest, but I guess he probably knows already.

The phone is ringing again when I get up to the house. I grab it. It's Storm.

"Hey, what happened to you last night?"

"I went home."

"Sorry about that. I guess I had a little too much."

"That's okay. Did your parents find out about you stealing the car?"

"Uh-uh. They didn't even see me in there. They thought I was in bed. But here's the weird part: Someone stole my bike last night. They're pretty pissed about that."

"I did. How do you think I got home?"

"Oh, right. Hey, lemme go call off the dogs and I'll get back to you."

I hang up and dial Forest.

"Hey. I just heard."

"Is your mom okay?"

"She's great. She's had a Realtor here for hours. She's putting the house on the market. I know it's pretty weird but I think she feels like she's finally doing something right."

"Where will she go?" I ask quickly, selfishly trying to figure out how all this will affect us.

"I don't know. She's thinking about New Hampshire."

"New Hampshire? That's, like . . . far."

"Yeah, I know, but she's got a sister there and my grand-mother lives there too."

"Oh."

My dad comes in and stands in front of me gesturing that he needs the phone.

"I gotta go, my dad needs the phone. I'll call you back."

"Sure."

I hang up and hand him the phone. "Now can I have a cell phone?"

"We'll see," he says, punching numbers.

"It would make a thoughtful birthday present." I point to the calendar above the phone, displaying the month of August. The number thirty, my birthday, is circled in red marker. I tap it with my finger but my dad seems not to notice. I also glance at the quickly disappearing days till Forest leaves. It makes my stomach hurt to see that we're down to days instead of weeks now.

I notice my dad's cell phone is sitting on the table. I hold it up in front of him.

"It's not charged," he says, with the phone at his ear.

I look at the display. It's flashing "YOU HAVE A MESSAGE." I press the message button and it shows the number of the last caller. It's Forest's home number. My dad's too busy speaking Spanish frenetically to Reynaldo to notice what I'm doing. I place the phone back on the table and walk away.

It's difficult to say exactly how an entire town can know someone's private business in a matter of hours. I imagine the rumor mill at work: The receptionist from Funk, McIntyre, and Monk tells Carmen, her manicurist, while she has her acrylic nails filled. Carmen tells her brother, who works on a construction crew, and he tells everyone else on the crew, some of whom are Mexican, who tell their farmworker buddies. Once it hits the farmworkers, the news goes all the way over the border into Mexico and all the way back until everyone knows. As word of the settlement spreads like wildfire, my dad seems to have changed teams overnight. He now plays for the Mexicans again. I don't think that any of the workers ever believed that there was a hope in hell that Tomás could win this settlement, but now that he has, my dad has gone from rabble-rousing troublemaker to some sort of saint. I'm pretty sure that he won't have any trouble finding workers to help with the new root-vegetable garden anymore.

On the flip side, the ranchers and factory farmers are none too pleased with this news. They don't like the idea of any migrant farmworker thinking he has the right to sue over every little thing that happens. If he loses an arm in a thresher while working on their land, for instance, well, that's just his problem. I'm sure that they worry that things could get way out of hand if these people start feeling empowered. My dad has never been a favorite of theirs anyway, moving into the valley with all his fancy new ideas about organic farming and sustainability and generally stirring things up. I'm sure they'd all be happy if he just disappeared.

Meanwhile, all the usual suspects have reappeared. Every newspaper in the area is buzzing around my dad again, wanting his opinion on the plight of the migrant farmworkers and the flawed immigration policies of this administration. The *San Francisco Chronicle* is even doing a big story on the case, with a side story exposing the abuse of farmworkers and the dangers they face crossing the border to find work. They want to interview my dad and they're coming out next week to take photos.

Steve and I make the drive over to Reynaldo's to fetch Tomás. This time I'm at the wheel the whole way. It seems to take about half as long as it did when we delivered him.

When we pull into Reynaldo's vineyard, Tomás is standing there with his little duffle at his feet. The wounds on his face have almost healed but otherwise he looks the same. It occurs to me that knowing he has some money coming doesn't really change the fact that he lost someone he loved. When he sees us he grins. I'm not sure I've seen him smile like that before. He's standing with an intense-looking young woman with fine features and long black hair. They seem to be saying good-bye like they wish they weren't.

On the ride home I can understand enough Spanish to know that Steve is giving Tomás a hard time about the girl, and he looks away, embarrassed. I pinch Steve hard on his bicep.

We only have one tiny driving episode on the way home when I pass a car on the one-lane road and then panic because I can't find fourth gear, but I finally do find it. I see Tomás crossing himself in the rearview mirror. It probably didn't help that I started screaming. It also didn't help that Steve was laughing at me.

When we arrive home my dad tells us that Uncle Ned worked his magic on the insurance company and he managed to extract one hundred and fifty thousand dollars from them. Most lawyers would take a third of that as their fee, but Ned only wants ten percent to cover his costs. The money will be slow in materializing, so Tomás will be with us for a while. Considering what everyone went through, this might not seem like a lot of money, but to Tomás it means the difference between a good life and one of endless labor and risk-taking. It will buy a future for him and Rosa and probably his extended family and his in-laws.

Steve goes into the kitchen and gets busy on his famous enchiladas, a Mexican homecoming dinner for Tomás. I stand next to him and whip up a big bowl of guacamole with fresh avocados and limes. The mood is festive and we joke around a lot. My dad puts an Eddie Palmieri CD on the stereo. He's Puerto Rican but it seems to work. Miguel and Tomás run into town for a case of cervezas and when they get back a toast is made in Spanish, something about prosperity and friends and those who have passed.

After dinner Steve pulls me out of my chair and we two-step across the linoleum in our bare feet. I'm an awful dancer but Steve's had a couple of beers and he seems not to notice. Rufus barks at our feet. I look over at my dad watching us. He's smiling and he nods at me. I'd forgotten what it feels like to be held in the gaze of a parent like that.

I look at the clock above the sink and leave the boys in the kitchen as the volume of their conversation increases. I wander onto the porch with Rufus and sit cross-legged in the swing watching darkness settle onto the farm. The buildings and fence posts become shadowy and a cool breeze mingles with the warm air, scenting it with sweet grass. The chicken coop has been repaired and the chickens are calm again, as chickens go.

Rufus pricks up his ears at a pair of headlights coming

up the drive. His tail thumps three times and a low growl gathers in his throat as he IDs the visitor. When Forest opens his car door, Rufus leaps down the porch steps, tail wagging, and gives him a proper welcome.

Forest walks slowly toward me and I try to figure out if he's nervous. I decide that he probably isn't. As weird dads go, mine is about neck and neck with his, maybe just a hair ahead.

I take his hand and pull him into the brightly lit, noisy kitchen. The boys stop their animated Spanish and give Forest a hearty, loud welcome. I introduce him to my dad and Forest leans across the table to shake his hand. There's a certain amount of sizing each other up but my dad is pretty cool about the whole thing, offering up a chair at the table and asking if he's eaten. There's a half-eaten casserole of enchiladas sitting on the counter. Forest eyes it hungrily and I make him a plate. He digs in and the conversation resumes. I can see him following the Spanish floating over his head, trying to catch threads of it. He'll be fluent before long. I make a promise to myself to learn too. Over the summer I've picked up a lot, but if I tried harder I could be part of this conversation. I sit down next to Forest and he smiles at me and squeezes my knee under the table. Rufus curls up on the wood floor with his head on Steve's bare feet, completing my ragtag little family.

20

$\mathcal{O}$n the last day of my summer with Forest, which is also the eve of my birthday, Storm stands behind me and ties the long white apron at my waist. Then I do hers. Somehow she manages to make her apron look sexy. I look like I work in a basement morgue at a hospital. Forest is wearing a white apron too. He looks like he works with me at the morgue. We're part of the volunteer waitstaff at the second annual Field of Greens dinner, another one of my dad's brainstorms. The miles-long white-tableclothed dining table runs between two rows of organic cornstalks in the middle of a cornfield. The guests are locals and out-of-towners, all of whom have paid one hundred dollars a plate to taste the bounty of all the organic and sustainable farms, vineyards, and ranches in the area. The farmers, ranchers, and vintners who contribute to the dinner get in for free, and famous chefs from San Francisco, Berkeley, and a few other places are invited to participate by preparing one course each. All the food is prepared in a big tent with generators humming behind it to power the stoves. The profits go to support Field of Greens, my dad's sustainable farming group. It pays for advertising and educational programs and the rest goes into a fund to help support starting farmers or suffering farmers or whatever else comes up.

Millie, from the diner, is in charge of us and she hands us each a bottle of white and a bottle of red wine.

"Red goes in the round glass and white goes in the taller one. Please don't mix them up. Oh, and no sampling!" She looks at Storm when she says this.

We head to our sections. Forest walks next to me and Storm falls behind. She sees something worth taking a second look at in the form of a tall dark waiter.

"This is a breeze," says Forest.

"Yeah, talk to me in four hours when we're pouring coffee and serving dessert."

As we pour the wine, another group of waitstaff, volunteers from the participating restaurants, brings out the first course, an amuse-bouche made from local goat cheese with peach chutney and caramelized leeks, served in a leaf of endive. The waiters carry massive trays, and the plates are miraculously delivered in a matter of minutes.

My dad is sitting next to Reynaldo and his wife, Maria. Steve, Tomás, and Miguel sit across from them. Connie Gilwood is sitting way down at the other end of the table. This must be my dad's doing. Tomás doesn't know who she is. My dad hasn't arranged for her to meet him yet and tonight is certainly not the night for an "I'm sorry I killed your wife" talk. Connie is sitting next to a friend of hers, a woman I recognize from town. She has high hair and long nails and gold bangles that announce her every move. She's carrying a handbag large enough to fit a toddler. She's probably a Realtor. She's probably selling Connie's house. Connie is wearing a long, flowing lavender cotton skirt and a plain white T-shirt. She has silver hoops in her ears and her hair is pulled back in a ponytail like the last time I saw her. A few loose strands fall across her thin face. The effect is quite pretty. She appears to have given up the Heather Locklear look for good. Maybe it wasn't attracting the right people. In this deconstructed version of Connie Gilwood I can see a bit of Forest in her eyes and around her mouth.

We whisk the empty plates away and new trays of food magically appear, loaded with cups of chilled cucumber and dill soup with crème fraîche from an organic dairy near here. We refill the wine and water and clear endless plates as course after course is delivered. The table is full of appreciative diners and there's a lot of oohing and aahing.

As I'm clearing my section I'm noticing that my dad

is heavy into a passionate conversation with Reynaldo, and Tomás is leaning in too. He appears to be involved in whatever they're talking about. I'm curious to know what it is but I'm too busy to go over there and see what's going on. Steve is entertaining a group of city women, his regular Ferry Plaza Market customers. He no doubt charmed them into buying tickets. I can tell that he's deep into the wine already. Nothing pleases Steve more than free wine and lots of women. Jane, who's working with us, watches him and rolls her eyes at me.

The main course is finally served on big platters, family-style. Roasted ears of corn rubbed with chipotle butter, links of chorizo sausage made from pork and grass-fed organic beef, barbequed chicken, roasted artichokes with romesco sauce, potato croquettes, and stuffed bell peppers. As soon as we set down the platters, the servers fill their own plates in the tent and we sit in a circle and dig into the food that's been making our mouths water for almost two hours.

A band wanders onto the small makeshift stage carrying their instruments. They look like they might have started hitchhiking in Mississippi about four days ago. There's a stand-up bass player in a porkpie hat, a washboard player/drummer, and a hangdog guitar player. They start in with some old Hank Williams tunes, the perfect accompaniment to a country dinner. I heard that Uncle Ned, who looks nothing like a lawyer and everything like a banjo player tonight, is going to sit in later. Storm is sipping from a pink plastic tumbler of white wine and she's getting pretty cozy with the tall dark waiter. Watching her, it occurs to me that Storm might start to feel very old when she actually reaches the age that she tells everyone she is now. It's like she's robbing herself of her own youth. She sees me watching her and winks at me.

The sun starts to dip in the sky and the smell of sweetgrass and cornstalks fills the air. Forest and I sit next to each other, eating without any table manners. He's never experienced anything quite like this and he's taking it all in like a Boy Scout on a field trip. After every bite of food he makes a comment and then after a while he just groans with pleasure. He's never tasted food like this. I brush some hair out of his eyes and look at him with so much love that I must look like I'm going to burst. I start to think about him leaving. He reads my mind and shakes his head. I've told myself that every moment till he leaves has to mean something (with time out to go to the bathroom and sleep a little). I want him to leave here with a head full of memories, enough to last him till we see each other again. I'm having trouble imagining my life here without him. I snap a photo of him shoving a forkful of food into his mouth. He's become so used to me taking photos that he barely notices.

I take one of Storm too. It's hard to get her when she's not posing. She sticks her tongue out at me.

As the main course is cleared away, my dad gets onto the stage and talks a bit about Field of Greens. He brings all the chefs and their staff out from the tent to cheers and wild applause, then he gets all the waitstaff to stand, more applause, and then he says a few words about the people who dig and haul and plant and weed and do all the backbreaking work to get this wonderful food to the table. There's only a handful of workers at the table but my dad makes them stand up and the table claps for them. Storm whistles like a sports fan and we all cheer for Tomás, Miguel, and Steve.

Dessert is served: strawberry and peach shortcake and plates of lavender shortbread and meringues. The only thing we're serving that didn't grow here is the coffee. We walk around the tables with big thermoses but most people are out of their seats by now and the band is playing again. Ned is up there with his banjo and people are waltzing politely in the grass and gathering in small groups. The volunteers join the party and someone lights tiki torches next to the band and lanterns on the table as darkness closes in on us. The kitchen is lit by the generator-powered lights and we pile up all the dishes in there until Millie tells us that our work is done. I look around for Storm and see her making a discreet exit into the cornstalks with Tall Dark and Handsome. Forest and I grab hands and take off like schoolkids at dismissal time.

The path goes for a quarter of a mile till we come to the field where all the cars are parked. We jump into Forest's car and bump along the field watching the bugs fly at our headlights until we find the main road. Then we barrel down the road to the tar pits. The car knows the way. When we get there, Forest turns off the engine and kills the headlights but he leaves the stereo playing. There's a blues CD on. The sound of it puts me in a strange mood. The water looks thick and oily in the dark.

Forest turns to me and grins. "You're probably wondering why I've asked you here tonight."

"I asked *you*, remember?"

"Oh, right. What for?"

"I wanted to discuss the economic situation in subSaharan Africa," I whisper, "among other things." I take my camera strap from around my neck and hand my camera to Forest. He leans over and puts it on the backseat.

"Right. Other things." He runs his hand along my jaw the way he always does before he kisses me. His hand smells like the awful pink soap from the sink in the tent. He presses his lips against mine and I move in a little closer. I feel my body responding to him but I'm all instinct, like a cat. The real me is in the backseat, watching, fascinated.

Forest runs his hand from the small of my back to my bra strap. I'm wearing the only nice bra I own, a soft pink lacy cotton thing that Storm made me buy "on the outside chance that anyone would ever see it," she explained. Storm owns lingerie that comes with directions. I'm guessing that she's helping Tall Dark and Handsome remove it right now.

I arch my back as Forest's hand explores my body. He pulls gently at the hem of my skirt, revealing my bare, tan legs, which look to me very unlike the legs he's been looking at all summer in my cutoffs. Somehow they're part of a different package now. All the scrapes and bruises and Band-Aids are invisible in the moonlight and they look long and sensuous and new.

When I envisioned having sex with Forest (and I have a million times), I didn't see how things would simply move along toward it like this. I imagined a more clinical setting with a lot of discussion about what we were going to do next. I imagined Forest reassuring me that it wasn't going to hurt and that I shouldn't be afraid, but none of that is happening. I'm not at all afraid. My hands are moving over his body on their own. They seem to know what to do and where to go. Our kissing is long and deep and as natural as breathing. We seem to share a tongue and our lips are exactly the same temperature. The kissing sends an electric charge through my body all the way into my toes. Forest gently pushes me back on the seat and I struggle out of my skirt, a little awkward but manageable. He pulls my tank top over my head and looks at me before he kisses my belly and my chest. I pull at the straps of my bra and he undoes the clasp. (Storm highly recommended the front clasp for this very purpose.) I'm naked now except for my panties and I'm grateful for the darkness because they are nothing to write home about. I unbutton his shirt and help him out of it. I throw it into the backseat, where the real me is still sitting, impressed as hell.

The rest of our clothing somehow disappears from our bodies and we're skin-to-skin for the first time ever. I feel him against me and marvel at how something can feel so hard and so soft at the same time. The words I'd heard to describe it always made it sound like a weapon to me, something made of cold, hard steel, something to be feared. Forest rifles through the glove box for a condom and, I have to admit, it's awkward. All action stops while this weird little gelatinous thing is produced and put on. It's like the person you're about to have sex with suddenly decided to grow some sea monkeys and they just happen to have a package of them in the glove box.

Forest tells me that he loves me. It's like he knows I need to hear it before we go any further. My hands pull him closer, closer than we've ever been.

When it happens, I suck in my breath and hold it. There's a resistance inside me and then there isn't. It does hurt a bit and then it doesn't. I feel like Forest and I are working toward morphing into one being and then the connection is complete. I start to breathe again. I'm surprised when a tear rolls down my cheek. Forest sees it and kisses it away.

"I love you," he says again. He lies next to me on the seat; our bodies are warm and the air is warm and we hang on tight to each other. I don't want him to move. He doesn't.

"Are you okay?" he asks.

"I'm great. It was so emotional. I didn't expect that."

"Neither did I," he says.

"But you've had sex before. Wasn't it like that?"

"No. Everything is different with you. It's us. We're different."

"Better different?"

"Yes, better different."

"Hey, you wanna go swimming?"

"Yes."

"We don't have a towel."

"I have an old blanket in the trunk."

We jump out of the car and run naked, laughing, across the tiny beach. I hesitate a moment when I see the black bottomless water but Forest splashes past me and then turns back and grabs my hand. I follow him in. The water is only slightly cooler than the night air. I wrap my legs around Forest and we bob in the water.

"You're not going to fall in love with some potato-growing farmer while I'm gone, are you?"

"Maybe. What kind of potatoes are we talking about?" I smile.

"I don't know if I can bear being away from you. It could kill me."

"Me too. How tragic would it be if we both died from missing each other?"

"I hope it doesn't come to that." Forest looks up at the moon. "Hey, I wonder what time it is?"

I look up too. The moon is yellow and almost full, a harvest moon, they call it. "I don't know, close to midnight, I think."

"It's your birthday."

"I forgot all about it."

"Happy birthday."

"Best birthday ever."

"Best summer ever," says Forest.

"Best everything ever."

"Run away with me," he says.

"Okay, soon."

Forest drives me home and in the driveway I hold on to him as tight as I can. I don't want to get out of the car but I do, bit by bit, coming back to him several times for one more kiss. I finally close the car door and drag myself up the porch steps, feeling like a rag doll.

The party has moved to our kitchen and my dad and Reynaldo are going at it, having sampled a lot of wine. Tomás is with them too. Maria's gone home. She's too wise not to have brought her own car.

I slip upstairs. I don't want them to see me. My hair is wet, my clothes are rumpled, and I feel years older than the last time I saw these people. I'm sure they'd see it too if they looked at me. I make it to the bathroom and lock the door. I pull off my damp clothes and run hot water into the old tub. I slide in and lay there, watching a water drop cling to the faucet and then lose its grip and fall into the tub with the others. I run my hand along my sixteen-year-old body. I feel changed. I'm not the girl I was when summer began. I've had sex with someone (someone who's leaving me in a matter of hours) and I've fallen in love. In a few days I'll have a driver's license. Are there any other birthdays as life-altering as sixteen? Are there any other birthdays that set you free like this? I don't think so.

I think about my mom and how excited she'd have been for this day. She'd want to talk about it openly and in full detail. I don't feel that lump in my throat that I've felt so many times when I think about her missing another rite of passage in my life. This time I feel calm and confident that I did what I did for all the right reasons. I did it because I love someone and he loves me back.

Rufus finds me as I'm leaving the bathroom with a towel wrapped around me. I close my bedroom door and pull a tank top over my head and then I change my mind and take it off. At sixteen one should make substantial changes in the way one lives. I'm going to sleep naked tonight and maybe forever. The sound of laughter and slurred Spanish still carries up the stairs but it doesn't bother me.

Rufus curls up on the rug next to my bed. He seems okay with the new me. He seems to like the idea that I've moved from the backseat into the driver's seat and I've taken hold of the wheel.

I drift off thinking of nothing but Forest: Forest's hands, Forest's lips, Forest's body, Forest's heart.

21

*M*orning washes over me later than usual on my birthday. I finally wake up exhausted and exhilarated. I'm surprised at my nakedness until last night's events come back to me. My dad's still sleeping. I heard him climbing the stairs at four a.m. as I was drifting between dreams and consciousness, both featuring Forest. All night, I kept flipping through a stack of mental photographs: where our hands were and when; what he said to me and what it meant; what was playing on the stereo; the way he smelled; the way he felt. It's ironic that I've spent my whole life snapping photos of the things I want to remember and here I am, having to recall what happened on the most important night of my life so far, frame by frame, without any visual aids.

I throw back the covers and pull on my ugly underwear

and yank a T-shirt over my head. I pad across the wood floor to the window. Jane and Steve are in the midst of concocting a birthday message of some sort with balloons and crepe paper. I quickly step back from the window. I don't want to ruin the surprise. The phone rings and I grab it.

"Hello?"

"It's me," says Forest. "Happy birthday."

"Hi. Thanks. I just woke up."

"I know. I'm parked in your driveway. I saw you in the window."

"You haven't been there all night, have you?"

"Don't be silly. I've only been here for a couple of hours. Good to know that 'up at dawn' crap you've been feeding me all summer is a big lie. Don't come out quite yet, okay? I'll call you when we're ready."

"Okay." I go into the bathroom and brush my teeth and look at myself in the mirror. I try to find the new me somewhere on my face but I don't look much different except for slightly bluish circles under my eyes from lack of sleep, and puffy lips from all-night kissing. I go back into my room and pull on some jeans and slide into a pair of flip-flops. The phone rings again.

"Okay, now you can come out," says Forest. "Meet me at the front door."

As I open the screen door, Forest appears. He kisses

me and blindfolds me with a bandana that smells like patchouli, which means it belongs to Jane. He leads me by the hand down the porch steps and across the yard. I can hear Rufus trotting next to us and Jane and Steve giggling like children.

"Ready?" asks Forest.

"Uh-huh." He lets go of my hand and unties the bandana.

Jane and Steve are standing in front of a shiny new car, one of them on each end.

"Ta-da!" they yell.

It's my dad's old abandoned Mercedes, which has been sitting in the garage for the last two years, but it's been given a makeover. They washed all the bird poop off of it, waxed it, pumped up the tires, evicted the pigeon that was nesting in the passenger seat, polished up the chrome, and shampooed the upholstery. It looks brand-new. They also have it decked out like a parade float with flowers and balloons and a big banner that says "Happy Birthday, Roar!"

Steve dangles the key in front of me. "Check it out, birthday girl. This baby now runs on biodiesel."

"Mine?"

"All yours."

I take the key and hug him. "Can I start it up?"

He stands aside and gestures at the car like Vanna

White. He pulls open the driver's-side door and I slide into the seat. I insert the key into the ignition and turn it. The engine roars to life. I smell French fries. Jimi Hendrix starts to play.

I stick my head out the window. "Where'd the stereo come from?"

"Jane and I got it for you. Can't have wheels without tunes."

Forest is watching all this, beaming. I get out of the car and hug Jane too.

"Thank you, guys. It's the best birthday gift I ever got."

"You can fill it up with Millie's deep-fryer oil for now but she's putting in a biodiesel station in the fall."

"Can I drive it?"

"Stay on the property or your dad'll kill me."

"Get in, Forest."

Forest gets in the passenger side and I push in the clutch and find first gear. I let the clutch out slowly and give it some gas. The old car eases forward stiffly.

"She runs like a top. I tuned her up myself," calls Steve as we pull away. He and Jane stand there, beaming.

Forest grins at me. "Okay, here's the plan: We rob a 7-Eleven on the way out of town, and head for Canada, okay?"

"Sure." I give it more gas and shift into second. The

chickens hurry out of our way as I steer the car along the driveway. The balloons flap in the breeze and the crepe paper blows off in pink and blue chunks. The banner falls off and I run over it.

"Hey, good thing you've got a car now. George wants the beast back and I have a feeling it won't be here for me when I come back next summer."

I put my foot on the brake. The car stalls. "Wait, what?"

"Yup. I talked to your dad. He said I could work on the farm next summer."

"He did?"

"Well, Tomás and Miguel and Steve put in a good word for me. They said I was a good worker, which, yes, is an outright lie, but I'll learn."

I lean over the gear shift and wrap my arms around him.

"Hey, I'll miss that car," I whisper in his ear.

"Me too. Best time I ever had in a car." He smiles. "Forget the car, best time I ever had, period."

I start the car again and drive it back to the barn. My dad's up by then, hungover, and mad as hell that they didn't wait till he was up before they gave me the gift. He gets over it when I tell him how much I love it. He beams and takes all the credit.

Jane has a big country breakfast all planned out and she goes inside to get it together. Tomás and Miguel give me a big bouquet of wildflowers fit for a beauty pageant winner, which I put in a glass canning jar on the kitchen table since we still don't own a vase.

Forest and I take off down the path through the field to the Cathedral of Trees. Forest has his book bag slung over his shoulder and I have my camera. When we get there, we sit side by side on a log, looking up at the light streaming through the trees.

"Promise promise promise me you'll come back," I say, still looking up, afraid to meet his eyes, afraid I'll cry. I feel so fragile.

"C'mon, I promise," he says, pulling me closer.

He flips open the book bag. He pulls out a gift wrapped in tissue paper printed with little daisies on it and hands it to me. It makes my heart ache to think of him carefully wrapping it for me. I tear the paper off. It's a book of photographs by Elliott Erwitt called *Elliott Erwitt's Handbook*. I flip through it. The photos are all black-and-white candids. All of them are of people expressing themselves with their hands, people from all over the world. Inside the front flap, in Forest's tidy handwriting, it says: *She handed me an apricot . . . Happy Birthday, Love "F"*

"It's beautiful. I love it." I kiss him on the cheek.

"I have one more thing for you." He digs back into the book bag and comes out with one of his journals. He hands it to me.

"What is it?" I look at the untitled cover.

"It's the diary of us. Starting from the first time I saw you and ending at today. You can read it when you need to know how I feel."

I flip through the pages and stop somewhere near the front. I read a paragraph. Forest uses the same brown ink for the entire book. Something about that touches me.

I saw her again today. Pretended it was an accident. She was selling vegetables at the farmers' market. Her hair was pulled back with a rubber band. I got nervous, didn't know what to say. GOD, what an idiot! So uncool. I think I told her something about her eyes. She looked at me like I was full of shit. I told her I was sorry about Sylvia but it came out all wrong. How will I find her again? Can I leave it to chance? She's so beautiful, so calm, so watchful. She hates me, I'm sure of it.

I look up at Forest. "Are you sure you want me to have it? It's so private."

"Yes. I want you to have it. I'm not embarrassed."

"Okay. Thanks." I'm so moved by this gesture but I try again not to cry. It's too early in the day for that. My eyes fill with tears. I blink them away.

Forest takes my camera from around my neck and looks through the viewfinder, playing with the focus. He takes several shots of me, sitting on the log, holding his gifts, missing him before he's even gone.

Back at the house, Jane has pancakes and eggs on the grill, bacon and veggie sausage frying, and hash browns sizzling. My dad has the espresso machine fired up and he's making two coffees at a time. Steve is setting the table with cheesy party hats that say "Sweet Sixteen" on them at each place and balloons are tied to the back of my chair. The kitchen is noisy and smells beautiful. Dr. John is on the stereo playing New Orleans jazz piano.

Forest goes outside to call Miguel and Tomás in to eat and we sit down at the table, passing platters of food and talking with our mouths full. This is our last meal together as a family. Jane will help Steve pack up his things tomorrow and head back to Berkeley for the beginning of fall semester. Forest will be gone in a few hours, and my dad informs us that he has some news: Tomás has made a life-altering decision. Reynaldo has asked him to come over to his vineyards as his apprentice, working directly under him. He's offered to help get him started in the process of becoming an American citizen, and with the money he'll be getting from the lawsuit, he'll be able to afford a down payment on a small place and bring Rosa back from Mexico. Wanda will live with them and take care of her during the day. How does all this stuff keep happening right under my nose and why am I always the last to hear about it?

We toast Tomás's success and then everyone sings "Happy Birthday" to me followed by "Las Mañanitas," the song they sing at Mexican birthday parties. Then we toast to the end of a great summer growing season. For the fall and winter it will be just my dad and Miguel and me. We'll hire day labor as we need it but there's a lot less to do on the farm after the summer's over. We'll still do the markets and the restaurants but soon we'll be selling root vegetables, pumpkins, and winter greens like kale and chard. Steve will still work the Ferry Plaza Market with my dad to make some extra money but my dad will pick him up in Berkeley on the way. The chickens lay a lot less in the winter so we'll only sell eggs on the roadside stand and maybe a few dozen a week to Millie.

One of the things that you learn when you live on a farm is that change comes at you whether you're ready for it or not. Every season is punctuated with its own smells and tastes and you find yourself looking forward, waiting for the next thing to come along so you can take a bite of it. When we lived in the city, this marking of the seasons didn't seem to happen to us. We drifted from one season to the next without thinking about it too much. This life is very different. It's so much more than putting on a sweater or grabbing an umbrella. It's about setting your internal

263

clock to the sun and the moon and the seasons. The longer I do it, the better I understand it. It's not something you can teach. You have to live it.

After breakfast we pile the dishes next to the sink, all sticky with maple syrup. Forest has to catch a flight to L.A. from Oakland at two p.m. so I walk him to his car. I hang on to him for dear life. I practically break his ribs and it's still not enough. This isn't a summer romance. This is us, forever, as far as the eye can see. When he finally pulls away I touch my finger to my cheek and taste our tears. I can barely stand to watch him drive up the road. Rufus licks the salt from my dangling fingers and distracts me from what I'd really like to do, which is lie right down on the dusty ground and howl. Instead I take Rufus up to my room, crawl under the covers, and open Forest's journal to the first page. I read it as I run my finger along the Guatemalan bracelet that's been tied to my wrist since the day Forest gave it to me:

I saw a girl today in a hospital waiting room . . .

22

*C*onnie Gilwood gets a decent offer on the house the day after she puts it on the market. A man who runs a tire store in Stockton and his wife and two kids will move in at the end of September. They're moving up in the world. Connie is leaving in two weeks for New Hampshire. She's going to live in her sister's guesthouse until she finds a place of her own. She's downsizing.

My dad keeps his promise to her and arranges a meeting with Tomás. When he asked Tomás if he would do it he wasn't crazy about the idea (who would be?) but he eventually agreed to it. Connie doesn't speak Spanish so my dad translates. It happens at our kitchen table, which is fast becoming the place where all important exchanges occur. I stay out on the porch, cross-legged on the swing, but I can hear as much of the conversation as I need to. Connie doesn't try to offer any excuse for what she did. I give her credit for that. She humbly asks for Tomás's forgiveness and Tomás gives it to her. He tells her that Sylvia forgives her too and that's when she falls apart. I hear her sobbing and then I hear a chair scraping across the floor and I know that Tomás has stood up and gone over to her. I'm sure that he must be hugging her or touching her somehow; I know that this will only make it worse for her because I've seen that look in Tomás's eyes and I know that it's a powerful thing.

When it's over, Tomás goes back to work and my dad walks Connie to her car and they say good-bye. Her eyes are red and the skin on her face looks raw. I suppose that this meeting with Tomás will help her move on. I suppose I'm glad for her. After all of the horrible things I've imagined about her, she doesn't seem like such a bad person anymore. It's obvious that even with Tomás's forgiveness she'll regret this for the rest of her life.

Steve and Jane are already gone. They're on their way back to Berkeley in Steve's loaded-down Jeep to start school again. I'm out of my mind with missing Forest even though he only left yesterday. I walk down to the mailbox for something to do, and even though I know it's impossible, I'm hoping there will be something from him, something tangible to accompany the three emails he's already sent today. I pull out the *New York Times* for my dad and a stack of bills, plus two birthday cards, one from each grandmother, each containing a check for fifty dollars. At the bottom of the stack is a large

envelope addressed to me. The return address is *FOTO* magazine in New York. I tear it open right there on the road:

> *Dear Ms. Audley:*
> *Congratulations. On behalf of the editorial staff, the*
> *judges, and everyone here at* FOTO *magazine, I am*
> *happy to inform you that your photo titled "Reluctant*
> *Rodeo Clown" is the winner of this year's FOTO*
> *magazine photography award.*
>
> *Please read the enclosed release carefully, sign it at the*
> *bottom, and return it to our office by September 15. Your*
> *photo will appear in the November issue of the magazine*
> *and a check for ten thousand dollars will be forwarded to*
> *you upon receipt and acceptance of your release.*
>
> *The* FOTO *magazine contest winner is*
> *painstakingly chosen from thousands of entries both*
> *national and international, professional and amateur.*
> *Your work was found to be exceptional and you should*
> *be very proud. Please contact me if you have any*
> *questions.*
>
> *Sincerely,*
> *Meg Barton*
> *Associate Editor,* FOTO *magazine*
> *Brooklyn, New York*

I stand there on the road dumbstruck. I'd completely forgotten about the contest. There was so much going on and I really didn't think I had a chance of winning anyway. After I sent my entry off, I looked online at all the past winners and they were all hot-shot photographers with interesting names and interesting lives.

I read the included release form. There's a space for me to write a short bio about myself. I remember that I lied about my age on the contest application. Will it matter to them? Should I come clean? I practice the conversation I'll have when I call Meg Barton, the woman whose name is at the bottom of the letter:

Hi, this is Aurora Audley, the photography contest winner. You know how I said I was twenty-one on the entry form? Well, I'm actually only sixteen. In fact, I just turned sixteen YESTER-DAY! So, how about it, can I still have that ten thousand dollars?

Oh, brother. I look at my watch. It's twelve thirty; that's three thirty in New York. Well, I suppose now is as good a time as any. I walk back up to the house and drop the rest of the mail on the kitchen table and go up to my room and shut the door. I call the number on the letterhead.

While the phone is ringing all the way in New York, I remember something else. Back when I called the subscription office, the woman on the phone told me that it was sent to me by someone in Key West, Florida. It was my mom who got me the subscription to the magazine. I wonder how she knew I was still taking pictures. Was a magazine subscription supposed to be some sort of parting gift for being such a good contestant in her little game where we pretended to be a family for twelve years?

"*FOTO* magazine," says a woman in a crisp voice with a hint of a European accent. I picture her in a slim wool skirt and heavy black-framed glasses that make her look über-smart.

"Hi. May I speak to Meg Barton, please?"

"Who may I say is calling?"

"It's Aurora Audley. I'm the photo contest winner. I—"

She cuts me off. "I'll put you through."

"Meg Barton speaking." She sounds all business too, but more New York, brusquer.

"Hi, um, this is Aurora Audley, the photo contest winner."

"Ah, Miss Audley. Congratulations."

"Yeah, thanks. It's about that. Um, you know on the entry form where you ask for the person's age?"

"Yes."

"Well, I might have exaggerated a little."

"Really? By how much?"

"Well, I'm actually sixteen."

"Wow, you are?"

"Yeah." My heart starts to sink.

"Can I ask you something?"

"Sure." My heart sinks further.

"How long have you been taking photos?"

"Since I was six."

"I'm sorry. Did you say six?"

"Uh-huh."

"Well, don't worry about the contest. There's no age requirement. You just need a parent to sign the release. You do have one of those, don't you?"

"Sure."

"But, let me ask you this. How much work do you have like the photos you sent us?"

"Tons."

"Really?" She seems to be considering this. "Listen, I'm about to go into an editorial meeting but why don't you call me next week and we'll talk about your work a bit. I may be able to help you get what you need."

"What I need?" Did I miss the part of the conversation where I said I needed something?

"Yeah, like an agent, a scholarship, a gallery, stuff like that. I assume by the quality of your work that you're not just dabbling here. You do want to be a photographer, don't you?"

No, I want to work at McDonald's. "Yes, of course," I answer quickly.

"Well, call me on Monday morning. I'll talk to some people in the meantime and see what I come up with. Okay?"

"Sure, thanks!" I click the phone off.

TEN THOUSAND DOLLARS! TEN THOUSAND DOLLARS! I fly down the stairs and out the front door, where Rufus joins me, galloping at my heels. The chickens scatter, scolding us. I'm still grasping the letter from the magazine in my hand. I look around for my dad and I finally see him toward the back of the property, talking to Miguel, wearing a wide-brimmed straw sun hat.

"Dad!" I call, but he doesn't hear me. I keep running along the raised beds, through the apricot orchard, and past the fig trees.

"Dad!" He finally turns around and watches me racing toward him. He looks anxious at first; that kind of yelling usually means a farm accident, dismemberment, exploding plumbing, approaching tornado. When he sees my face he relaxes his into a smile.

"Dad!" I stop in front of him, gasping for breath. I hand him the letter. He reads it quickly.

"You won?"

"I won!" I gasp, trying to catch my breath.

He quickly tells Miguel in Spanish; he chuckles and nods at me.

"Roar. This is fantastic!"

"I know. It's ten thousand dollars! I won ten thousand dollars! And guess what?"

"What?"

"She wants to see more of my work. She thinks she can help me get an agent and stuff like that."

My dad's face darkens a bit at this news. I know that he's several steps ahead of me. He's thinking about the day I have to leave this place. He's already imagining the farm without me. He forces a smile.

"C'mere." He opens his arms and hugs me hard, lifting my feet right off the ground.

"I'm so damn proud of you," he says, meaning it.

"I gotta go call Forest," I say, turning on my heel and running back the way I came.

"Hey, Roar!" he calls. "Use my cell phone. It's charged." He holds it up.

"It's private," I call to him, running backward for a few seconds. He shrugs and puts his phone back in his pocket. Something about that gesture makes me sad. Maybe I should have taken his phone just to make him feel like I need him.

Forest wants details: Which photo? Which issue will it be in? What will I say in the bio? Who did I talk to? Exactly what did she say? He's the kind of guy who needs details to make things real. He's so happy for me he could bust. I really wish he were standing next to me for all of this.

"What'll you do with all that money?"

"I don't know, probably use it for school; it's not like I have a college fund."

"There's a lot of good photography schools in New York, you know."

"I know."

"We could be roommates."

A warm rush flows through my body. I love it when he says things like that.

"We could." I love that he's so sure of us.

The next day is registration for eleventh grade. Registration is a deeply unpleasant experience. There's always the endless lines to stand in for the issuing of lockers, textbooks, and class schedules, while being forced to listen to returning students describing their pointless summers. The smell in those hallways is something you won't soon forget: rotting sneakers, floor wax, and wet paper towels. Storm is picking me up and we're going to knock it out together and then go directly to the Department of Motor Vehicles so that I can take my driver's test. I've practiced on the Mercedes, which is a stick shift, so taking the test in her mom's car should be a breeze.

Storm honks the horn from the driveway at nine a.m. and I dash out of the house and hop in. She's wearing a minidress in a Pucci print and my mom's white go-go boots.

"So what's this news that's so important that you won't tell me on the phone?" She slides her sunglasses to the top of her head and leans in to examine me closely. I think she even sniffs the air. "OH MY GOD! You've had sex!"

I blush and look away. "Is it that obvious?" Where, exactly, is she seeing it on me?

"To me it is." She puts the car in gear. "Welcome, honey. It's about time. Wow, it's just so refreshing not to be driving around with a vestal virgin in the car. That was getting old. So how was it?"

"Um, great. That's not the news, though."

"It's not?"

"Well, it's news, all right, but it's not THE news." I tell her about the photography contest and she's happy for me but I can see that the sex news figured a lot higher on her list of priorities. When I'm done telling her all the details she looks at me dead seriously and says:

"You leave me behind in this hellhole of a town and I swear I will never forgive you, Aurora Audley, do you hear me? NEVER!"

"Okay." I change the subject. "Hey, it's okay that I'm

using your mom's car, isn't it? I mean you did ask her, right?"

"Sure I did. But she's over at the church all day working the Jesus Bingo so she won't even notice that it's gone."

So I'm off to get my driver's license in a potentially stolen car.

"Do you have the insurance card? They need to see that."

"Check the glove box."

I flip it open. Inside there's a pocket-sized black leather-bound Bible, a rosary, and a hymnal.

"Wow, it's like the road to salvation in here." Storm's silver flask is sitting on top of the pile. "With a pit stop in hell." I wave the empty flask in front of her.

"Thanks, I was looking all over for that thing." She takes it and drops it into her white vinyl bag.

I spy a little pink card poking out from under the Bible and pull it out. It's an insurance card. I check the date. It's current. "Okay, we're in business." I slide the card back in under the Bible and close the glove box.

"Oh, I almost forgot." Storm rifles through her bag. "Here's your birthday gift." She hands me a small jewelry box. I open it. A perfect pair of silver hoop earrings are nestled in the cotton.

"Wow. These are gorgeous. They're not from the family jewel collection, are they?"

"Don't insult me. They were purchased from a reputable jeweler named Tony."

I put them on. Storm twists the rearview mirror toward me so I can see myself.

"Check it out. They're fabulous."

She's right. They're the most grown-up jewelry I've ever owned.

Along the main road before the school turnoff, a giant-sized Brody Burk head smiles down at us from a billboard. Underneath his photo it says "Brody Burk for Congress—Leadership You Can Count On." He's wearing the same black cowboy hat he was wearing that day he threatened me.

"Brody Burk is running again?" I ask Storm.

"Sure. He's whipped up plenty of support in this county too. What, did you think he'd give up? No way, sister. Let me tell you something about small-town living. The more things change, the more they stay the same."

"Thanks for putting things in perspective for me."

"Don't mention it."

As we sail past the billboard, I notice that someone has climbed up there and spray-painted the word "asshole" on the pocket of Brody's fancy western shirt.

We pull into the school parking lot and Storm parks in a spot clearly marked "Faculty." She has a way of parting the waters and somehow we get through the lines in record time. Storm stops at the mini-mart for a five-gallon cup of coffee to go with her "ciggie" and we drive the twenty miles to the DMV with Storm coming dangerously close to scalding her bare thighs with every sip of hot coffee. Meanwhile she fills me in on the tall dark waiter from the Field of Greens dinner.

"His girlfriend, Carla, kept calling him on his cell phone, asking when he'd be home."

"And he kept answering it?"

"Yeah, I finally took it away from him and shut it off, but by then I'd lost interest so I sent him home to Carla. I think they're perfect for each other. City boys are so complicated. Who needs 'em?" Storm suddenly realizes what she's said. "No offense."

"None taken."

We arrive at the DMV with time to spare and I write the test and pass with only two mistakes. I took driver's education online and I actually remember most of the information I considered as useless as algebra back then. My appointment for the driving test is at one p.m. and Storm settles into the waiting room with an old copy of *People* magazine. The test only takes about fifteen minutes. I screw up on the pulling away from the curb part and my parallel park is far from perfect but the examiner isn't interested in spending any more time in Storm's smoky car and she grants me a temporary license. The real one will come in the mail.

After a photo, fingerprints, and a lot of paperwork I emerge victorious from DMV prison, waving my license. Storm drops her magazine on the veneer coffee table.

"Awesome! Now all you need is a fake ID."

She throws her bag over her shoulder and we exit the waiting room, leaving behind a vapor trail of Storm's signature perfume and a lot of disapproving head shaking.

The ride home feels very Thelma and Louise. You never know how a rite of passage is going to make you feel until you emerge on the other side, and having a driver's license makes me feel like hitting the open highway to search for the true meaning of life. We do this for roughly twenty miles but then Storm has to get the car back. When I arrive home the farm feels deserted. My dad's doing deliveries and Miguel and Tomás are at work on the new garden at the back of the property.

My brand-new provisional permit says I can't drive with anyone under twenty in the car at night, but by daylight, I'm free as a bird. I find the key to the Mercedes on the hook next to the back door and I walk out to the porch. My car is sitting there in front of the barn like an old, dependable workhorse, waiting to be called to duty. I walk over to it, open the door, and slide in behind the wheel. I turn the key in the ignition. The engine catches and the car comes to life. The odor of French fries fills the air. I find first gear and ease my foot off the clutch, pressing down on the gas simultaneously. The car rolls forward. Rufus watches wistfully from the front porch as I drive past it. The chickens scramble out of the way. The stereo starts up. Frank Sinatra sings "Fly Me to the Moon," a souvenir from Forest. I laugh out loud as I roll down the window and let the cool breeze blow through my hair. I steer the car to the end of the driveway, look both ways, turn the wheel to the right, and head down the road toward the horizon.

Acknowledgments

Heartfelt thanks to Charlotte Sheedy, Susan Rich, Meredith Kaffel, Alex Green, Ed Greer, Gail Wadsworth, Andrew Smith, Joe Henry, Gonzalo Villeblanca, the Amoeba Dream Team, and Dave (really sorry about the Post-its all over the kitchen table).